PHOENIX

FORCE

THE PREQUEL

Susan Horsnell

USA TODAY BESTSELLING AUTHOR

Contents

Author of Amazon No 1 Best Sellers in 2018:

Matt – Book 1 in The Carter Brothers Series

Clay – Book 3 in The Carter Brothers Series

Amazon No 1 Best Seller in February 2019

Andrew's Outback Love – Book 1 in The Outback
Australia Series

Amazon No 1 Best Seller in July 2019

Ruby's Outback Love – Book 2 in The Outback
Australia Series

Amazon No 1 Best Seller in May 2019

Eight Letters

Amazon Best Seller in April 2020

Cora: Bride of South Dakota

PHOENIX FORCE

The Prequel

Copyright © 2022 by Susan Horsnell

Written by Susan Horsnell

Edited by Word Pro Writer

Line Edit by Robyn Corcoran

Proofread by Leanne Rogers

Cover by Virginia McKevitt – Black Widow Books

https://www.facebook.com/blackwidowbooks/

A word from the author

This book is purely a work of fiction, a product of my imagination.

AILINIA is a fictional country and should not be assumed to be factual.

I have dramatized the mission and weaponry used to enhance the storyline, it is not to be accepted as fact.

The compound obstacle course and firing range are based on those used by the US military, but I have again taken liberties with these to enhance the storyline.

Claire Marshall transitions from being a serving, to a retired Lieutenant Commander, and keeping with the practice within the US Navy, she is at times addressed at the senior rank of Commander.

While this story does contain some facts, it remains a work of fiction and should not be taken as truth.

I hope you enjoy this introduction to the Phoenix Force series.

Sue

Prologue

AILINIA

Four and a half months earlier

CLAIRE

My left knee was tucked beneath me, my right leg bent out in front with the foot flat on the ground. A Colt M4A1 Carbine assault rifle rested on one shoulder, my hands steady as I stared down the scope, unblinking.

I watched the village beneath, as well as Ali Akbar Jabbar, a formidable terrorist who never hesitated to execute innocent victims.

SEAL team 3-Naval Special Warfare Group, which I had been a member of for almost five years, was tasked with shutting the asshole down and bringing his reign of terror to an end.

He and his lackeys had slaughtered thousands throughout the country, most recently an entire convoy of US men and women who had been transporting much-needed supplies to an outlying village. They had been ambushed as they made their way through a narrow canyon and hadn't stood a chance.

The US Government, thanks to the outcry from the public, had at last been forced to do something about the mad man—one of many, but by far the worst, and it was about fucking time. They'd been sitting on their hands for far too long.

We no longer needed Jabbar alive. Pity, I would have loved the opportunity to torture the bastard, but his second in charge had been captured a few days earlier and sang like a canary. The powers that be in Washington would be analyzing the information for months, if not years.

This was our team's fifth tour of the God-forsaken country. This mission had lasted almost two months and we had only been home from the last one—where we had been gone almost a year, for a month before being sent out again. Something I was grateful for, I'd needed to get away from the States for a while.

Thanks to solid intel we'd received, we finally had the prick, whose life I wanted to bring to an end more than any other, in our sights.

Jabbar stood in front of a seated Malik—an elderly man. Jabbar's rifle was trained at the innocent man's forehead while the rest of his men circled him, holding back the villagers who were begging for the old man's life. I could see Jabbar was rapidly losing patience with the situation and held my breath, waiting for the instruction to take him out.

A clear shot was presented when Jabbar stepped off to one side to speak to one of his men.

I knew the rest of the team was waiting for word from our leader, Commander, Doug Cartwright, Codename—Tiger, before any of us could make a move.

"I have the shot," I whispered, knowing the team would hear me but no one else.

"Hold steady." Doug's command surprised me, this was the first chance we'd had to take the fucker down and we had been waiting for hours. Why was he delaying?

"Tiger?"

"Hold steady, Wolf."

I flexed my front leg, which was beginning to cramp, before moving it back into position and continuing to stare down the scope of the rifle.

Four hours had passed since I'd set up on a hill covered in low bushes. The position not only gave me a clear line of sight but also prevented me from being discovered.

The rest of the team were situated in equally strategic positions, but as the team's number one sniper, with a hit rate of ninety-nine percent, I'd had my choice of location.

Jabbar now paced back and forth in front of the old man while he spoke on the phone. He was becoming angrier by the minute, and if he continued to pull at his hair the way he currently was, he'd be bald in no time. It was fortunate he didn't need hair where I was about to send him.

"Tiger?" I tried again.

There was silence from Doug, and a feeling of dread slithered down my spine, causing goosebumps to break out over my flesh. Sweat dripped into my eyes, the salt burning before I blinked it away.

"Stand down. Recon, Alpha 2."

I couldn't believe what I was hearing and remained frozen in place. Numerous expletives exploded over our communications channel; none of our team could believe we had been stood down at such a crucial moment.

Not one to disobey a direct order, I lowered my rifle, dropped to my stomach and began shimmying backward.

That was when yelling erupted from below and I stopped to witness what was happening. Jabbar threw his phone, cursed loudly in Dari, lifted the machine gun and fired numerous shots into the old man's forehead.

My stomach turned over as the Malik's head exploded, sending blood and brain matter spewing in every direction. Screams filled the air, men and women dropped to their knees, but what happened next had my blood turning to ice.

The sound of machine-gun fire filled the air and men, women, and children were mowed down in a hail of bullets. When the smoke cleared, Jabbar and his men were gone, and all that remained were dozens of lifeless bodies.

Suddenly, the decision I'd been wrestling with for more than a month became easy. My tour was up, and as soon as I reached stateside, I would be handing over my discharge papers and leaving the Navy.

I was tired of suits in Washington making decisions about situations they knew nothing about and costing lives.

I looked back at the lifeless, unmoving bodies. It was a shameful day for the US Military and those who had made the decision for us to pull back. Those in charge had a great deal to answer for.

Having no need to stay hidden, I stood. Jabbar and his men were now long gone. Looking down at the carnage below, I made a vow to those innocent beings—I would return and exact revenge on those responsible for their murders, and there would be no one other than me calling the shots. No mercy would be shown.

~*~

I stormed up to where our team leader waited in the compound and stood toe to toe with the man. Although I was tall at five feet, ten inches, Doug towered above me. I stood with my head tilted back and was sure the anger I felt showed on my face. Being second in charge, the rest of the team depended on me to get answers when something was stuffed. Instead of heading to their quarters and unpacking their gear, they all lingered nearby.

"What the fuck was that all about?" My hands were tightly fisted on my hips as I spat the words at our leader—my superior... For now.

"Commander, stand down." Doug turned to walk away, something I was not about to let happen. I moved to block his path of retreat.

"No, I will not stand down....*SIR!* We need answers about why we were pulled. I had a clean shot and I want to know why we were recalled."

My superior sighed and dragged a hand over his bald head. "I don't like it any more than you do, Claire. Orders came from Washington and you can bet I'm going to demand answers as to why we were not permitted to proceed as planned." I could see he was almost as angry as me, but he managed to hide it a lot better. "Two months of contradictory intel and chasing him all over the fucking desert, and then when we do catch up with the asshole, we have to sit and watch an entire village of innocents being slaughtered. As soon as I get answers, you *will* be the first to know." He glanced at the rest of his team. "You will *all* be the first to know. For now, our tour is up and we've been recalled."

"I'm sorry, sir. I know it wouldn't have been your decision. It's just so fucked up and I'm done. As soon as we step stateside, I'm leaving the navy behind. I can't continue with my hands tied in this way." I was sorry about how I had spoken. Doug and I had been friends for years and taking my anger out on him was unfair.

Doug nodded in understanding. "If I don't get a satisfactory explanation, I'll be joining you in telling my superiors to get fucked."

With a nod to each other, we let the matter be for now, and while Doug headed for the communication's tent, hopefully to get answers, the rest of us made our way toward the mess tent.

~*~

Stateside, One Week Later

If I'd thought the clusterfuck in Ailinia had been bad, it was nothing on what I was about to be confronted with when finally back on US soil.

I descended the steps of the military aircraft, my duffle bag over one shoulder, and was immediately approached by Admiral Ross Lessing. I wondered if he had heard about my argument with Doug and the news I'd officially resigned my commission. *Four days.* I had four days before civilian life claimed me, and the navy wouldn't see me for dust.

Stepping closer to the Admiral, I snapped to attention and saluted. "Sir."

"Follow me, Commander."

Fuck. If the serious tone of his voice was any indication, I was in a whole world of trouble. As we walked toward the administration building in front of us, my mind shot back to the news Doug had given us two days earlier.

"Commander, gather the team and meet in my office in five minutes." Doug strode off without waiting for an answer.

It took only a minute or two before I'd gathered the team and we reached the rendezvous point.

The flap of the small tent, which Doug used as his office, was thrown back, and our leader was seated at his desk. A scowl of anger I had never seen before crinkled his handsome face.

After ushering the rest of the men and women inside, we stood waiting for Doug to speak.

He raked his eyes over the six of us as he dragged a hand over his head. It was obvious he was agitated and I suspected whatever he needed to say would not be good.

"I've heard back from Washington and they gave me the reason for our stand down at the last minute."

"Which is?" I questioned.

"An Ailinian Minister, Abdul-Alim Aleem, in the interim government convinced the other ministers that taking out Jabbar would cause instability to an already fragile government. When Washington contacted the Ailinians and informed them we had our target in sight, they insisted our mission be abandoned."

"You have got to be fucking kidding me." I had *the mouth of a below deck sailor when I was angry.* *"So, you're saying they are condoning the slaughter of innocent people just so their positions in government are protected? And our pathetic people back home didn't tell them to get fucked? Fucking pathetic."* Did I mention I had a foul mouth when I was angry?

"Commander Marshall! I'm warning you to watch your language when speaking to a superior and show respect for the Ailinian leaders."

"Or what? You'll have me tossed out on my ass? Oh wait—too fucking late—I quit!"

I had stormed off before Doug could say another word, my anger had been overwhelming. I had barely spoken to him again before flying out. Along with the rest of the team, he was staying on for another few days until the replacement team had arrived and were briefed. For some reason, I had been recalled immediately and figured I must be in some pretty deep shit.

The admiral held the door to his office open and indicated for me to enter. A female officer, who had been seated, stood when I stepped inside and offered a smile. Her eyes swam with...was it sympathy? She offered her hand and introduced herself as Lieutenant Commander Andrea Maxwell. After rounding his desk, the admiral indicated for us to be seated and then seated himself.

"Sir, can I ask what this is all about?" Why was I recalled before the rest of the team? Is it because I submitted my resignation from the Navy?"

The man stared at me closely for a moment. His somewhat pitying expression had me wondering if I had jumped to the wrong conclusion. But if my argument with Doug wasn't the reason I was now seated before Admiral Lessing, then what was?

"Commander, I have asked Andrea to join us as she is a navy psychologist who is well respected for her approach in situations of loss."

Loss? I felt impatience creeping in on me. Surely, they weren't going to force me to attend counseling when my tour of duty with the navy was at an end? If they insisted, it could delay my transfer out. I noticed the admiral swallow hard a couple of times, and my confusion grew. Was he nervous?

"Commander...Claire. I am so very sorry to have to be the one to break the news, but two days ago, your parents, brother, and sister were killed when a truck being driven by a drugged driver ran a red light. They died instantly."

I was frozen in shock. The admiral had to be lying. My parents and siblings were the only family I had in the entire world. There was no one else. No aunts, uncles, cousins. Mom and Dad had been only children of only children. The loneliness of their lives had been the reason they'd had the three of us.

No! The admiral was wrong. My family was safe and well in San Francisco. When I fixed my eyes on him, I saw the truth in his.

Screaming filled the office, I had no idea where it was coming from though. The person sounded tortured, just as I felt.

The psychologist dropped to her knees, a pair of strong arms wrapped around me, and I was held close against her chest.

"I'll leave you both alone. Take as long as you need." Moments after the admiral spoke, I vaguely noted the door to the office opened and closed.

I drew back and stared at the officer's face. "Please tell me it's not true." Tears streamed over my cheeks, and even as I begged the woman holding me to tell me a mistake had been made, I knew it wasn't the case.

As if in a daze, I pushed her away and stood. "I can't do this; I need to get home."

As I reached for the door handle, she moved to my side and slid a card into my hand. "If you need to talk with someone, I'm here for you."

I nodded but had no intention of getting in touch. After leaving the office, I negotiated my way along the halls until I reached outside.

The sun was high in the sky overhead, the sky as blue as the ocean. Why was I noticing such things? I hurried to the main gate, flashed my ID card at the sailor on duty, and, not waiting for his salute, hoisted the duffle bag higher onto my shoulder before setting off at a fast walk in the direction of home.

~*~

Home was a spacious modern apartment on the fourth floor of a building that was a five-minute walk from the base. I'd moved in a month before my final deployment, shortly after Ty and I had ended our relationship.

[18]

I held back the tears which threatened to fall, but once I stepped through the door and into the familiarity of my living room, the dam walls burst.

I dumped the bag on the floor where I stood, dropped to my knees, and cried harder than I had ever cried in my life.

I was alone. I'd lost everyone I loved, and after fifteen years of serving my country, I was out of a job. Was there any point in even trying to continue living? Why did a murderer like Jabbar get to survive while my family, who had done nothing wrong, were snatched from here on earth?

I curbed my instinct to scream and shout at the injustice of it all, not wanting to have concerned neighbors turn up on the doorstep, or worse, call the police. I had no desire to explain I was broken. Raw. And at that moment in time, truly believed I had no reason to continue on living.

Chapter One

Two months after returning from Ailinia

Once my parents, brother, and sister had been laid to rest, I hadn't allowed myself to wallow in grief. Instead, I set about making the ideas that had consumed my mind become a reality.

I finished showing the two men over the compound, a property of two hundred and sixty acres, and we were back in the computer room located in the basement of the warehouse building.

"Sign here." I scribbled my signature on the line Alain Cook—CIA operative, mission manager, and long-time family friend, from San Diego indicated. He then flipped to the next page and I signed again. I lost count of the number of pages I scribbled my signature on while Alain and General Craig Simmons, my Washington contact, supervised. Once done, the papers were separated into two different piles, and we all shook hands.

The general spoke first. "Good luck with putting your team together, Claire. Ensure they each sign off on all conditions and make it crystal clear that once they join the team, they no longer exist as far as the US government is concerned. Miles Williams is my computer expert in Washington, and I'll discuss possible candidates with both him and Alain and have him drop a list in your secure email later today. He'll be available if you need anything and will fly out to induct your computer expert when ready. Once you have chosen your members, all hard copy information must be destroyed. There can be no record of them and their pasts."

"I understand."

"I congratulate you on this compound, Claire. I must say I'm both impressed and a little jealous." Alain took another look at the bank of computers surrounding where we stood.

The equipment in the room was state of the art and whoever was chosen to fill the position would want for nothing.

"I can't thank you both enough for all your help."

"Remember, in, out, and remain dark at all times." The general hadn't needed to remind me, I was well aware that it was crucial we fly under the radar. "Your parents would be extremely proud of how you have used some of the proceeds from the sale of your family's business."

"Thirteen billion dollars certainly goes a long way to achieving one's dreams, but I would give all this up to have my family back." I fought back the tears that burned my eyes.

"Yes, all the money in the world won't replace them, but you have us. If you need anything at all, you know how to get in touch. Now, it's time we left you to get on with building your team. Once you have everyone in place, we'll meet again." Alain kissed my cheek.

He had been the first person I'd gone to with my idea as he'd been a close friend of my father for over thirty years. He had been the one to take it to the general. Both men had been more than willing to help, on condition they weren't given detailed accounts about me, or the rest of the team, in case anything went sideways. I'd had no trouble agreeing.

I escorted both men out and returned to the warehouse.

~*~

Before I headed to visit with my best friend, Hannah, who had moved into the area after marrying, I took one last look over the compound. It was now finished and ready for the team.

The main building was an enormous warehouse structure, set well back in the wooded area of the grounds, away from prying eyes. At ground level, the entry door opened into a large kitchen that boasted the latest cooking technology and gadgets. I couldn't cook if my life depended on it, one of the drawbacks of growing up in a wealthy family—we'd always had someone Dad paid to do it all for us.

Upper and lower cupboards filled three walls, and in the center of the room was an island bench with six high back bar stools positioned on each side. There was enough room to pass by on either end to reach the sink and the main area of the kitchen. A massive window offered views of the Anza-Borrego Desert State Park, which shared boundaries with the compound.

The kitchen opened onto a living area which filled the rest of the ground floor. White leather couches and bean bags were positioned throughout, offering seating for eighteen to twenty people in comfort. On a brick feature wall hung a home cinema-sized television screen, beneath it sat an entertainment unit with all the latest in gaming technology and a library of games.

On the far end were four powder rooms, two on each side of an elevator. The sliding doors off the living room opened onto a deck that led to a swimming pool and hot tub. There was also a separate building off one end that housed a fully equipped gym–vital for maintaining fitness.

Views from the elevated deck were over the compound. Both the pool area and the kitchen had a fully stocked wet bar. One of my rules would be that no one over-indulged, we never knew when we would be needed for a mission.

I stepped into the elevator, which led to the floors beneath but didn't stop at the next two. The first I shot past housed my personal suite and eight self-contained suites for team members. Each of the eight had a living room, a kitchenette for late-night coffee or a snack, and a bedroom with an ensuite bathroom. The next floor I descended past housed another ten suites.

When the elevator reached the basement, I stepped onto the floor, which was my pride and joy— the command center, or war room, as some would prefer it was called. I had spared no expense, investing in all the latest military and civilian computer technology and surveillance. I took my time admiring the setup for about the hundredth time since it had been installed.

Four giant screens were positioned on one wall, and below them was a shelf with eight smaller screens. In a semicircle around the room were another twelve computer stations. All screens were opaque and had touch technology or could be used with a keyboard. It was the operator's preference.

In the center of the semicircle was a large table for strategic planning. This also had touch technology and would be vital in planning missions. The entire area was like stepping into an interactive computer game that took up two-thirds of the floor.

The other third housed another four powder rooms, two flanked each side of the elevator, and a large conference table sat sixteen people. Nearby, a locked concrete-surrounded, freestanding room housed all our weapons—a large selection of handguns, sniper rifles, machine guns, knives, flashbangs and grenades. My team's personal choices would be added as the members arrived.

Satisfied that everything was in place for this stage of my venture, I stepped back into the elevator and pushed the button to take me back upstairs to the ground floor.

I didn't tour the outside as time was getting away, and by the time I negotiated the ridiculous security, which both Alain and Craig had insisted on having in place, I would barely make it to Hannah's on time.

I left the building knowing it was secure and made my way to the 'mom' car I drove—a black Chevrolet Equinox. As much as my heart craved the dream vehicle—a black Mustang, my head insisted having one would draw unwanted attention. I also figured none of the team would travel in such luxury, which wouldn't be fair.

I climbed into the vehicle, secured my seatbelt, and headed for the first gate to begin the exit procedure.

~*~

When I pulled into the driveway and glanced around, I noticed how gorgeous the gardens looked. The lawn was lush and healthy, the shrubs and trees bursting with color.

After unclipping the seatbelt, I stepped from the car and grabbed my overnight bag before heading to the entry door. Various perfumes from flowers hung in the air, the combined scents were divine.

"Claire! Oh my God, you're finally here." Hannah jumped up and down when she opened the front door to find me standing on the front porch. She stepped forward and I was squeezed in a bear hug. "It's so good to see you, it's been way too long."

It had been over a year before I'd left for Ailinia since we had last seen each other. Far too long. I hugged her back before drawing away.

"It's good to see you too, is Jared home?"

"No, he was called into work at the last minute on some important case, so it's just you and me until dinner."

She threaded her arm through mine and drew me inside. I parked my bag just inside the door.

"You look well and I'm so jealous of your gorgeous tan. Are you happy to be free of the navy? What will you do now?" The questions rolled over one another.

"As I said on the phone, I've been busy setting up my own security company about an hour from here. Dad's business was snapped up as soon as I put out word it was up for sale, which gave me the capital to invest in my own company. I'll be looking for employees over the next few days and will then be able to accept cases."

"Sounds exciting and I know you will enjoy being your own boss."

"I certainly will, and I'll be free to pick and choose which cases we take. I guess there will be a lot of cheating husbands or wives in my future." *Not fucking likely.*

I hated lying to my friend, but I would never be able to tell anyone outside the team what I really did for a living.

"Who's caring for the gardens these days? They look fantastic."

"I am."

"*You* are gardening? Since when?"

"Since I lost my job because of cutbacks. Jared said I didn't have to work if it wasn't what I wanted, and he would support me in any decision I made. I decided to stay at home because we want to try for a family."

I was sure my bottom lip hit the polished wooden floor when my mouth dropped open. This was Hannah. High-powered lawyer, Hannah. *"I never want kids."* Hannah. *"I'll be a Circuit Judge by the time I'm thirty."* Hannah. Had I fallen down a rabbit hole?

"I've been spending my time redecorating the house and gardening. A couple of times a week, I catch up with friends over coffee."

I was speechless. Never in a thousand years had I pictured my best friend as a suburban housewife.

"Say something."

"Um…"

"I knew you would be shocked, which is why I wanted to tell you in person. I was dying to see the reaction on your face, and you didn't disappoint." Hannah laughed.

Finally, getting my thoughts in order, like a battalion of soldiers on parade, I was able to speak. "I can't believe you gave up your dreams for a life as a wife and mother."

Hannah frowned. "What's wrong with being a wife and mother?"

I placed a hand on her arm. "Absolutely nothing, it just wasn't how I pictured you living your life after everything you have said over the years. I'm happy for you, Hannah if it is what you want."

"It is. It truly is. Now, come inside, and I'll show you what I have been busy doing while you have been trudging around the desert shooting people."

I followed Hannah through the cool of her air-conditioned home. She led me into the kitchen, as was our ritual when I visited, and I took a seat at the table while she grabbed a pitcher of iced tea and two glasses before joining me. We sat and chatted about recent happenings in our lives until Jared arrived home and spent the rest of the evening watching an adventure movie on television.

My visit was to last until after supper the following day, and I suspected once the time had passed, I would be more than ready to head home. Not because I didn't love my friend dearly, but because I detested predictable and mundane, and it appeared that was what Hannah's life had become.

"Is that place off the highway about an hour from here still operating? The one where they hire out horses for trail rides?"

Hannah squinted her eyes as she thought about my question. "Coyote Canyon Stables. Yes, I believe it's still operating. Are you planning on taking a ride?"

"I'd love to, it's been a long time since I've ridden." I closed my eyes for a moment. "Not since Jellybean passed away three years ago. I think a trail ride would be just what I need to relax before I go home and start organizing the business. What do you think, wanna come too?"

Hannah shook her head, and I felt the disappointment clear down to my combat boots that I wore everywhere.

"I can't, honey, in case I'm pregnant. I know it should be okay, but I don't want to take the risk. You go and enjoy yourself. I'd planned to have coffee with a couple of the ladies tomorrow, and I suspect you would rather go riding than join us and listen to gossip."

Never a truer word spoken. I would rather eat nails than join a bunch of gossiping women for tea. "Not my thing, as you know, so I will take a ride and should be back early in the afternoon."

"Wear a hat, it's going to be another hot one."

"I didn't bring one."

"I still have mine, which you are welcome to borrow."

"Thanks, I will." I found myself looking forward to a ride through the peaceful countryside, breathing in the clean air without having to wear a face covering to protect against dust and sand.

Chapter Two

Hannah was still in bed when I left the house. I couldn't comprehend how she could sleep until past 9 a.m. I left a note on the kitchen bench saying I would be back at around two and slipped quietly from the house, locking the door behind me.

The one-hour journey to Coyote Canyon Stables, which was back near the compound, passed quickly, and in no time at all, I was easing the car into a parking space beneath a tree. After turning off the motor, I slapped Hannah's hat on my head, left the car, and hit the button on the remote to lock the doors.

I drew in a deep breath, and smiled at the combined familiar scents of horse, manure, and leather that lingered in the air. I had been away from horses for far too long, and once the business was settled, I was determined to acquire a horse of my own.

Tucking the keys into a back pocket, I strode to a building where a white sign on the door read 'office'. A bell over the door tinkled as I pushed inside, and a girl greeted me from behind the counter.

"Good morning, I'm Beth. How can I help you?"

"I was hoping to take one of your horses out on a trail ride for a couple of hours."

She looked me up and down, scrutinizing my appearance. I was used to being looked over. I was tall for a woman, and although slender, I was well muscled. I'd dressed in faded jeans, my combat boots and a checked shirt. Hannah's hat, which I had removed on entering the office, was clutched in my hands.

"You an experienced rider?"

"Ridden all my life and competed until I joined the military."

She nodded, seemingly satisfied. "I'll put you on King, he could do with expending some energy. He needs a confident hand, but he's steady over difficult ground."

Beth laid a map open on the counter and pointed to the various trails marked in different colors that showed beginner to expert. It was kind of like how resorts mapped out their various ski trails.

"Do you need someone to go with you?"

"No, as I said, I have been riding all my life and would really appreciate the quiet if you don't mind."

"Of course." Beth reached beneath the counter, gathered papers, and slapped them in front of me. "Fill these in and I'll have King saddled."

I watched as she left through a back door before filling out the papers. They wanted the usual—name, address—I gave the address for my parent's beach house in Coronado, not wanting to answer unwanted questions. By the time she came back, all the i's were dotted, the t's crossed, and I was ready to get going.

Beth checked the papers. Happy that everything was in order and placing a great deal of trust in the fact I was telling the truth about being experienced, she invited me to follow her outside.

The property was impressive, well-maintained and cared for with pride. This was the kind of place where I wouldn't hesitate to board a horse. As I followed Beth across the yard to the stables, a rider in a large arena caught my eye and I stopped to watch.

Beth stopped beside me. "That's Nevada Phillips practicing mounted shooting. The lady is a crack shot and fast. I have no idea why she doesn't compete. I asked her once. She shrugged and said she was no longer able to participate."

I heard a beep, and the horse shot off, keeping low to the ground as it weaved and spun around barrels that had balloons floating above. The magnificent chestnut quarter horse was sure-footed, needing almost no guidance from the rider who used only her left hand for control.

Cracks of gunfire filled the air as Nevada lifted her right arm and fired. One balloon after another was hit dead center, sending pieces of rubber flying through the air. Once done, she guided the horse at a fast gallop over what I assumed was the finish line, and another beep sounded. She glanced up at the covered stands and nodded.

"Does she come here often?" I kept my eyes on Nevada while speaking with Beth.

"Yes, and her horse, Texas, is stabled here."

I took the information on board. I was on the hunt for two snipers other than myself, and if this lady was as good with a rifle as she was with a pistol, I was certainly interested in recruiting her.

As she slowed and noticed us watching, she shoved the pistol into a holster strapped to her thigh, led the horse toward the fence, and raised a hand in greeting. Beth and I reached the fence as Nevada reined Texas alongside.

"Looked like you rode a good time." I hoisted a leg over the enclosure, extended my hand, and we shook. "Claire Marshall."

"Nevada Phillips.' She glanced up at the time clock. "Not bad—14.79seconds." Turning her attention to Beth she said, "I need the boys to get more creative with the course, Beth. It's not challenging Texas or me." She patted the side of her horse, who had barely worked up a sweat.

"I'll let them know."

I heard the sound of a horse approaching from behind me and turned to see a young guy leading a majestic blue roan gelding who was at least sixteen hands high.

I kept my eyes locked on the beast as he approached. The muscles in his shoulders bunched as he plodded our way, pulling against the lead rope, wanting to run free. Swinging my leg back over the fence, I jumped to the ground. When the horse was close, I reached out and ran my hand over his muzzle.

"You taking King out?" Nevada sounded surprised. "I hope you have plenty of experience, he's a feisty one with a mind of his own. Even his owner refuses to ride him, and I hear he's up for sale."

I looked at Beth, who nodded, acknowledging Nevada was telling the truth.

"Get the owner on the phone and organize the buy."

"Are you loco? You haven't ridden him yet."

"I'm perfectly sane. I'll buy him at any price."

"Well, I won't tell him that, I'll get you the best price I can. I'll let you know when you get back from your ride."

"Thanks." I mounted up, and as I sat firm in the saddle, King pranced on his front feet, eager to be gone. I pulled back on the reins while rubbing a hand over his side to settle him. "Nice to meet you, Nevada, maybe you'll join me for a ride one day soon."

"I'd like that; good luck with King."

I slackened my hold on the reins, turned the horse toward the start of the trail, and kicked him into a gallop. With the wind whipping through my persistently messy hair and caressing my face, I finally felt as if I could once again tolerate life.

~*~

King picked his way along a narrow mountain trail; he was both confident and sure-footed. When we reached an open pasture, I gave him his head and he didn't disappoint. Muscles rippled beneath me as he gobbled up the thick grass beneath his hooves. He was strong with an even gait, and for a large horse, was remarkably light over the ground. My desire to own him heightened and I hoped that by the time we returned to the stables, Beth would have managed to convince the owner to part with him.

When the landscape changed to a steady slope toward the river, I slowed King to a walk and allowed him to go in the direction he wanted. It was clear he'd been in the area before.

As he plodded along, thoughts of Nevada filtered into my mind. The lady puzzled me. Her shooting skills were like none I had ever seen; she was both fast and deadly accurate. It was obvious to anyone with a pair of eyes that she loved the sport of mounted shooting and wasn't suffering an injury that would prevent her from riding or shooting. So why had she told Beth she was unable to participate in competitions where I was sure she would have left other competitors in her wake?

When King reached the river's edge, I soaked in the vista before me. The country in this region was spectacular and diverse—from lush forested areas to wooded mountains and bare deserts.

The wide river before me flowed with determined purpose, and lush pasture grass descended into thick river reeds, which lined the edge of the water. Hills rose from beyond the bank on the opposite side, reaching into the clear blue sky above. Birds flitted from tree to tree, chirping and whistling to each other. It was the only sound, apart from the rippling of the water. This was what I'd needed–the peace and quiet of nature.

King stepped through the reeds until he reached where the water ran clear. My feet remained just above the water, and I sat up straight in the saddle when he bowed his head to take a long drink.

Once he was done, there was no need to tell him what to do next. He raised his head, tossed his mane, and plodded back onto dry land.

I patted his side and gave him the go-ahead to start back. I could have stayed out there all day, but time was passing, and I wanted a spot of lunch before spending the afternoon with Hannah. In truth, I was also anxious to get back and find out if my offer on King had been accepted.

~*~

I dismounted and led King at a slow walk toward the stable block. There were two washdown bays attached, and I headed toward the only one not being used. I was surprised to find Nevada washing down Texas in the adjoining bay.

"I thought you would have been long gone by now, Nevada." I glanced at the watch on my wrist, confirming it had been more than two hours since I had seen her in the arena, and it was now approaching the time for lunch.

"I took Texas out on one of the easy trails. It gives him a chance to run without the constraints of the arena."

Nevada must have arrived only moments before I had, and we remained silent while washing the horses. Once we started brushing them down and could hear each other if we spoke, curiosity got the better of me. I began probing.

"You have Texas fully boarded here?"

"Yes, and he's cared for very well. I'm usually out here three or four days each week to exercise him, and one of the staff does it when I can't."

"How often do you practice shooting?"

"A couple of times a week. I can't compete anymore, but I do it because Texas and I love the workout. We've been together a lot of years."

"Why don't you compete? You looked outstanding, although I'm no expert on the sport."

I didn't miss the slight stiffening of Nevada's shoulders. The movement was minute, but as a former SEAL and experienced sniper, I had been trained to notice the tiniest of differences.

"Circumstances."

Her response was clipped and had an edge of finality, so I didn't push for more. I had the means to dig deeper once I returned to the compound. If Nevada was hiding something, it would soon become apparent.

We finished with our mounts and I followed her as she continued past the stables.

"Where are we going?"

She glanced my way. "To turn them out in that pasture, one of the staff will bed them down later this evening."

I followed the line to where her finger pointed at a large pasture that contained several grazing horses.

"King goes in there?"

"Usually he does, but I heard you tell Beth you wanted to buy him. I guess it's up to you whether you lock him in a stable or continue to leave him out."

The lady had sounded prickly since I'd asked what were probably personal questions. I got the feeling she'd prefer it if I left her alone.

Although alarms sounded in my head, warning me the lady was hiding a dangerous secret, my heart insisted she could do with a friend.

Hopefully, when I investigated Nevada Phillips, I wouldn't uncover anything too bad. I wanted the lady and her talent for shooting on my team.

After leaving King to run free, I said goodbye to Nevada, again mentioning we should catch up for a coffee sometime soon. I then headed to the office to speak with Beth.

Chapter Three

I was greeted by Beth when I entered the office, and when her eyes landed on me, she broke into an ear-to-ear grin.

"From the look on your face, I'd say you have good news about King. I've washed and brushed him down and Nevada showed me where to turn him out."

"Thank you for doing that, it's not something we expect unless you're an owner." She reached down, and when she straightened, placed a folder on the counter. "The owner has agreed to sell King and I didn't need to negotiate the price. I think you will be pleasantly surprised or shocked might be a more appropriate word. He didn't hesitate to agree to sell him. I really don't think he liked the horse, and if the number of times he was dumped on his ass was any indication, I'd say the animal didn't like him. How was he for you?"

"He was an absolute dream. Spirited but obedient. He's incredibly light on his feet for such a large beast. I think we're going to be great friends."

"I'm so happy for you both and I took the liberty of readying a contract for you. I'll fax it over to the owner once you have signed. Will you be boarding him here?"

"Yes, I'd like King fully boarded if you have the space. My job will take me away on a regular basis, but when I'm home, you can bet I'll be here with him."

Beth tapped the folder with a finger and I opened it to find out what I had paid for the magnificent animal with which I was fast building a rapport. When I sighted a sheet of paper on top showing the amount I'd paid for him, my eyebrows shot up into my hairline. Three times I reread the number. I honestly believed my eyes must have been playing tricks on me, or a zero had been left off the end. I looked to Beth for confirmation and found her grinning like the proverbial Cheshire Cat.

I pointed a shaky number at the figure. "Are you sure this is right? He's worth ten times this amount."

"That's what the owner said he wanted–five thousand dollars and the *"nuisance is yours"*–his words not mine."

I couldn't sign the papers fast enough, and after paying Beth the purchase price plus six months' board in advance, I left the office with a huge grin on my face.

Before climbing into my car, I glanced over to where *my* horse was leaning against a paint mare and sent a thank you to my parents in heaven above. I had no doubt they were still watching over me every day.

~*~

Before leaving the stables, I sat back in my car seat, grabbed a file from beneath the passenger side, and studied the information on the woman my contacts had recommended as our computer operative.

I had already perused the dossier, which briefly outlined Tiffany Meadow's past. Tiffany was the latest name she was using. So far, she was on track to manifest as many lives as a cat, and she was only twenty-five years old.

Even though her past wasn't detailed, there was enough to show she'd had a hard, confusing life for one so young. My gut told me she was who I wanted as part of my team, and I continued reading.

Left... no, she was pretty much kicked out of home, where she'd lived in a lower-class neighbourhood, at the age of fourteen, and she had ended up in a trailer park on her own. To fend for herself. I was impressed to note she had graduated high school with honors while working part time as a waitress at the local greasy spoon. After graduation, she'd changed her identity for the first time, applied, and was accepted to Quantico. Why she had left there so suddenly was a detail I hadn't been given. Cue another change of name and she had come full circle to again living in a trailer park. I flipped the page and continued reading. Currently, she waitressed part-time at a diner by the name of *Tasty Temptation* and worked a few private investigation jobs on the side.

According to General Simmons, who had strongly recommended her over three other candidates, she was now a hacker in competition with someone code named Bleacher—who was wanted by the FBI. Tiffany aka Andrea, was working on bringing him to justice.

The general had also included her handle—*Glinda.* It was what she used to conceal who she really was when online. I wondered about the relevance of the unusual tag, but that was her information to reveal, if and when she wanted me to know.

I took a last look at a photograph that had been included. The lady was a knockout with violet hair, eyes the color of the Mediterranean Sea, and it appeared she favored jewelry that referenced the flowers.

I set the file on the passenger seat, started the car, and backed out of the parking space. I was headed to Tasty Temptation.

~*~

I pushed through the door of the diner, which was the usual run-of-the-mill eatery that was somewhat in

[44]

need of updating, and clapped eyes on Tiffany immediately. She stood speaking with an elderly couple, and I took the opportunity to study her. She had an outwardly easy-going manner and a genuine smile.

When she noticed me by the door, Tiffany placed a hand on the woman's arm, and I heard her excuse herself before approaching me.

"Hi, lunch or coffee?"

"Both, thanks. Can I have a table in the back, please?"

"Of course." She peered around me. "You're alone?"

"Yes, I am."

"Follow me, please."

The diner wasn't busy, and she led me to a table in a back corner, which was out of earshot of other customers. I started to take a seat as she handed me a menu.

"Thanks, Andrea."

I kept my eyes on her as I spoke. As soon as I mentioned her previous name, she froze with her hand in mid-air, paled, and visibly stiffened.

"I would like to speak with you, if you have a few minutes to spare."

She glanced around. "I'm off in twenty minutes. Meet me at trailer 16 in the park across the street and we can speak in private."

"That's suitable. In the meantime, I would like an egg salad sandwich and black coffee."

Tiffany was looking at me with fear in her eyes, and I set a hand on her forearm. This woman appeared to be terrified of something from her past.

"It's nothing bad. I promise it's not my intention to reveal your true identity. I have a proposal for you."

She relaxed and her expression became one of curiosity. She gave me a tentative smile before heading to the kitchen to place my order.

Once she left, I settled back in the chair and opened my tablet to the book I was reading, taking the opportunity to relax. I knew once the team was in place, time to myself would be rare.

~*~

Half an hour after I had entered the diner, I knocked on the door of trailer number 16. Tiffany, dressed in a pair of faded jeans, flannel shirt, and wearing obnoxious blue cowboy boots on her feet, pushed the door wide and invited me inside.

A quick glance around told me the lady liked order in her life and had a fascination for anything to do with flowers, if the number of objects depicting every variety and color was any indication.

"Can I get you something to drink? Tea, coffee, water?"

"No, thank you, I'm fine." I indicated one of the two small couches opposite each other. "Can I sit?"

"Of course."

Tiffany's nervousness showed in her eyes, belying her confidence. I set the file from my hand onto a small table close by. Curiosity showed on Tiffany's face as she sat opposite.

"How do you know my real name? I changed it and moved across the country. There is no way you would have come across it by accident.

"It's a bit of a story. Will you hear me out?"

She nodded warily.

"You're a damn good hacker, one of the best, but not as good as one of the defense computer geeks in Washington." I paused when her forehead wrinkled.

"Why would a defense computer geek be interested in me?"

"I resigned recently from SEAL Team 3, sick of my hands being tied by red tape, and I'm now in the process of putting together a team of my own. I asked one of my contacts, a general in Washington, to do some digging and recommend a computer tech and other key people. I need people who are not only brilliant at what they do but who can keep their mouths shut. Your past at Quantico shows you can be trusted."

"I can't believe someone found me. I buried that shit deeper than Hell so my past wouldn't come back to bite me on the ass. I want to talk with him... her..."

"That all depends on the decision you make when I finish explaining."

"I want to know how my name and past were found."

"I have no idea. All I can tell you is; my contacts were instructed to pull names and they came back with four. The other three were former military and pretty damn good, but you're who I want."

"Why?"

"You have no family and no ties, which is a requirement for every member of my team. I'll explain in more detail if you decide you're interested in coming on board. Also, I'm told that during your time at Quantico, you were able to track criminals into the deepest recesses of the dark web. You located assholes the FBI had been searching out for decades. I'm convinced you're who I need for my team."

"Even though you know about my past?"

"*Because* I know about your past. You have overcome obstacles from a young age that most people twice your age couldn't. I believe you're the best, and I want only the best on my team."

"Okay. Wow. What would I be doing?"

"Digging in the web, finding assholes I want to put out of business. Permanently."

"Where would I be working from?"

"A compound adjacent to the Anza-Borrego Desert State Park."

"That's one hell of a walk from here every day."

"There are suites available at the compound, and one will be assigned for your use when you are required to stay twenty-four seven during a mission.

It will be yours whether you choose to stay full-time or not. You don't drive?"

"I can. I learned in my last year at school, but I can't afford a car on what I make as a part-time waitress and earn from the odd PI job." Tiffany looked thoughtful for a moment. "I'm in the middle of a case, so I need to stay here at the park for now. I don't mind the walk."

I shook my head. "Not happening. There will be times when something comes up and you may be needed in the middle of the night. It's not safe to walk. If you decide you're in, we'll discuss a vehicle."

"My current jobs?"

"The waitressing ends as soon as you sign the paperwork in here." I tapped the file with a finger. "I know about Carlos, and you can continue dealing with his case, but you will accept no other assignments from the agency."

"When would you want an answer?"

"Before I walk out of here."

"Wow, you don't believe in giving anyone time to think anything over."

"I'm offering you a position and the money to set you up for life. I don't have time to be jerked around. I have a priority mission to get moving on as soon as possible. If you say no, this conversation never happened."

"Can I ask one question?"

"Yes."

"Is this a covert, under-the-radar team? Will we be doing things that are illegal?"

I sighed. "That's two questions and the answer to both is yes. There is a general and a computer geek in Washington and a CIA agent here who will be the only three people who know about us, and if necessary, they will deny all knowledge of the team. If you join me, you will cease to exist. None of your friends can know what you do."

"I have no friends, but you would already know that. Can I keep my alias—Tiffany, I've gotten kind of attached?"

I nodded.

"I'm in."

I wasn't surprised when she accepted my offer even though I had given her very little information. Tiffany had everything to gain and nothing to lose. She was also smart enough to realize that fact. I watched her closely as she signed the papers I needed—the usual nondisclosure and vow to maintain secrecy, along with a bunch of documents the General and Alain had felt were necessary. Once done, she stacked them back in the file folder and pushed it toward me.

I placed my hands on the closed folder. "You got any plans now?"

"No."

"Good. Grab your wallet, and I'll show you where you'll be working."

We left the trailer, and I waited while she locked the door before leading her to my car. After we settled into our seats, I sent a text to Hannah, telling her I would be out for a couple more hours.

"Call the diner, Tiffany."

While she obeyed my request, I pulled onto the highway that led to the compound. At 60mph that was ten minutes down the road.

Chapter Four

Tiffany sat in the passenger seat with her mouth open and jaw dropped in surprise as she watched me go through the security protocol, which enabled me to enter the compound. When the second gate opened, I headed in the direction of the warehouse and pulled up alongside the entry door. After shutting off the engine, I turned in my seat to face my newest recruit.

"As you saw, security is tight, but once the entire team is finalized, it will go to a whole other level. We'll proceed with getting everyone access so you can come and go when you're needed. Cameras will record all movements, and you can pull up the tapes at any time." I placed a hand on her arm. "I have to make it clear, Tiffany, I am placing a great deal of trust in you. You will be the *only* person, other than me, who will have access to everything concerning missions and the team. Your confidentiality is essential. Lives will depend on you. I need you to tell me now—is my trust in you misplaced? Is there anyone anywhere in your life who could present a danger to my team?"

"No, absolutely not." Tiffany took my hand in hers. "Claire, this is a flippin' dream opportunity, one I thought would never happen. I give you my word, if anything presents itself which could place the team in jeopardy, I will immediately come to you."

"Thank you."

"Do I really have a choice but to be completely transparent? Don't you and your contacts have the ability to drop me in a deep hole, permanently?"

We both laughed, taking some of the tension and seriousness out of the situation.

"You must read too many spy books, Tiffany. Come on, let's get to business."

After giving Tiffany a brief tour of the ground floor, I showed her to the elevator and pushed the button to take us to the floor beneath – lower level 1.

When the elevator stopped and the door slid open, I indicated for her to go ahead.

This floor showed four white doors on each side and one at the far end, which opened into my suite. I led Tiffany to the first door on our right, pushed it open, and stood back so she could enter.

"The suites are all identical, and since you're the first to come on board, you get to choose which you would like. The floor below us is the same, but where the door at the end leads to my suite on this floor, downstairs there are two extra team suites."

Tiffany strolled through the suite that was decorated with a black leather couch and two matching chairs. A thick, red area rug sat beneath the glass-topped coffee table. A desk, bookcase, and state-of-the-art television and entertainment system completed the living room. The kitchenette was stocked with everything needed to create gourmet meals.

Tiffany stepped across the white marble tiled floor to open another door that led to a generous-sized bedroom furnished with a queen-sized bed. Red scatter pillows rested on the black-and-white duvet. Two walls had closets large enough to hold clothes, accessories, and shoes for two people. One end housed a safe where guns, knives, and other weapons would be kept locked away. On the opposite wall from where we stood, an opening led into a bathroom furnished in black and white with red accent pieces. The huge shower was fitted with massage jets to soothe an aching body after a mission, training, or gym session.

"This is... wow!"

"As I said, all the suites are the same, so it's up to you which you would like."

Tiffany thought for a moment. "The computer area is two floors below us?"

"Yes, the basement."

"Then, I would like the room directly below this one, which puts me closer to my workspace."

I scribbled the number on a notebook I held in my hand. "When we head upstairs, I'll give you a card with the code to your suite."

"Thank you." She ran her hands down the sides of her pants. I suspected she was both nervous and excited.

Knowing she would be anxious to see what she would be working with, we headed back to the elevator and I pushed the button for the basement.

When the door opened, I stood beside Tiffany so as not to miss the expression on her face when she first laid eyes on what would be her equipment.

Tiffany stepped forward; her reaction did not disappoint. "Fuck me!" She spun to face me. "This is what I have to work with? This is all mine?"

"The left side of the room with the four large screens fixed high on the wall, the smaller interactive monitors and control panels are exclusively for your use. The smaller desks and computers are for the team members. The interactive strategy planning table in the conference area is for use by everyone."

Tiffany moved closer to her equipment and danced her fingertips over the smooth surface of the control panel before spinning around. I noted the tears that had welled in her eyes but hadn't yet fallen.

"Thank you," she whispered. "This is beyond my wildest dreams, and I give you my word, I will not let you down."

"Welcome to the team. As soon as the other members are finalized, I'll take you all through the entry and exit protocol. I will ask General Simmons to have Miles Williams fly out from Washington to go through the setup with you."

"He's the one who found me?"

"Yes. He's the best the US has, but I have a feeling you'll steal that title away from him before long. So, lower level 2. We'll head back upstairs, and before I take you home, I'll set you up with a burner phone, laptop, pager, the card with the code to your suite, and temporary entry and exit protocol for the compound."

Tiffany stepped forward and tugged me into her arms. I stiffened slightly, not used to displays of affection from people I didn't know well. It didn't take long for me to relax and I accepted her embrace.

When she pulled away, she gave me a warm smile. "Thank you."

After logging her thumbprint and eye scan into the computer, we headed back upstairs. While I opened a safe in the wall and removed one of the phones, the code card, and one other items, Tiffany stood looking out over the compound. When I returned to her side, I saw the questions in her eyes.

"Once I have the entire team together, I'll show you over the rest of the place."

I held a credit card toward her, and she inclined her head, giving me a puzzled look.

"Buy yourself a car—one you have always wanted and don't worry about the cost."

"I can't do that, Claire."

"You can and will. My father was a billionaire many times over, and as your new boss, I insist you have what you need."

"My dream car will cost a fortune."

"Is that all?"

Tiffany laughed and shook her head. "Are you sure you're not crazy?"

I held my thumb and forefinger slightly apart. "Maybe a little, but not crazy enough to not know what I'm doing. Now, let's go, I have a friend expecting me."

Tiffany hovered nearby as I locked the door and we walked to the car together.

Ten minutes later, I pulled up to her trailer and left the car idling.

"One other thing, Tiffany."

"Yes?"

"It's fine for you to use the team computer to track down Bleacher. It might give you access to the areas you need to bring him down. Personal laptops, phones, tablets, and any other equipment are to be disposed of before you return to the compound. We can't have you being traced."

With a nod of acknowledgment and a smile, Tiffany climbed from the car. She stood waving as I drove away.

~*~

After spending the rest of the afternoon with Hannah, sharing supper with her and Jared, and promising I would visit as often as possible, I returned to my suite at the compound, made a coffee and settled into one of the recliner chairs in the living area with my laptop.

I flicked off an email to General Simmons advising him of Tiffany's decision to join the team and that she had signed the relevant paperwork.

I then composed one to Miles Williams, asking for his help.

Miles,

I need you to see what you can find on a lady who goes by the name of Nevada Phillips. She's around five-ten, five-eleven, shoulder - length blonde hair, hazel eyes, slim and fit. Around twenty-eight to thirty years old.

Nevada has professional level mounted shooting ability, or at least she does, in my opinion, and she speaks with a slight accent, which I suspect is Texan.

My gut says she doesn't have a background in the military, more likely a ranch girl and maybe she was in the police force? For some reason, she has relocated here.

I would appreciate any help you can give.

Claire Marshall.

I pushed the send key and sent the email over a secure line, which had been installed. Moments later, my inbox pinged, indicating an incoming message. I raised an eyebrow when I saw Miles' handle of *Bandit.* Surely, he hadn't found something so soon?

I opened the message and grinned.

Give me 10.

Relaxing back in the chair to wait, I cradled the mug of coffee in my hands after taking a few sips. My thoughts wandered to Tiffany. I could have asked her to investigate Nevada for me, but I wanted each of my team members to open up about any secrets they harbored in their own time. If they chose not to, that was their decision. It was information Tiffany would never receive unless volunteered. Miles had a way of locking her out of such information, and I was confident that even if she had the ability to break through, she wouldn't go looking.

Less than ten minutes had passed when I heard the familiar ping of an incoming email. Once again, it was Miles, and I clicked on the icon to open it.

Claire, info as follows:

Nevada Phillips, aka Sissy Evan Grant. You were right; she's from Texas and her father was a Texas Ranger.

Something about the name sounded familiar, but when I couldn't recall why, I shook my head and kept reading.

Sissy was a US Deputy before disappearing, presumed dead by authorities, after her father's death.

He didn't elaborate on why she had disappeared.

You were also right about her talent. The lady is an expert horsewoman and crack shot who competed in mounted shooting at the highest levels, leaving her competition in the dust. She hasn't competed since disappearing.

As requested, when we initially spoke, I have given you only need-to-know information but can assure you, there is nothing in her past which warrants concern, and she is deserving of top-secret, sensitive information clearance.

Nevada is trustworthy beyond doubt. She is honest, has integrity, and believes strongly in justice.

I have no doubt that she would make an excellent candidate for your team.

Bandit.

I hit the button to print off the information. Knowing she had been a US Deputy before suddenly 'going dark' would have given me reason to dismiss the intention of asking her to join the team if it had been brought about by some wrongdoing. Having Miles assure me she could be trusted indicated there was a valid reason for her disappearance. Like any of the others who might have questions in their pasts, whatever had happened was Nevada's story to tell if, and when, she was ready.

Satisfied I had potentially found my second sniper, I shut down the laptop, set it aside and picked up my phone. All I had to do now was get her to accept my offer.

After texting Beth to call me the next time Nevada was at the stables, I grabbed my tablet and opened the book I'd been reading. Tomorrow I would see about bringing more team members on board. I had given myself a month to get them all recruited.

Chapter Five

My first target two days later was a lady I was already familiar with, we had crossed paths on a couple of missions. She had been the leader of DELTA FORCE Team 3.

Jackie *Freya* Ross hadn't been on the list which had been emailed to me. She had sent me an email of her own saying she had heard on the grapevine that I was in town and would like to have a word. It seemed no matter how long you were away, someone connected with the military always knew when you were back.

I'd sent her a message saying I would meet with her this morning and was interested to know what she wanted.

I knew next to nothing about Jackie's past before she'd become the leader of a Delta Force team. I had met her when she had taken on a secondment to head up SEAL Team 5. Like many in the military special forces, she was tight-lipped about her history, and I had no reason to pry.

One thing I did know—she was one of the best shots I had ever worked alongside when our missions had crossed paths.

Standing only five feet, two inches, Jackie had hair as black as a midnight sky that she kept in a Viking type braid that was secured with a leather tie. Her eyes were crystal blue, almost silver. Freya was known to be stealthy, resourceful, and had extensive training as a field medic.

Her last mission with Delta had been FUBAR (fucked up beyond all recognition), and team members had been killed. She had almost been court-martialed when two members of the team had fucked her over by lying. Fortunately, the crew of the plane she had jumped from had presented a different, more convincing account—the truth, and Jackie had been spared.

The exoneration hadn't been enough for Jackie, the accusations by people she had trusted stung, and she had walked away from the military.

Currently, she had an office job, something I couldn't imagine her being happy doing.

Although we had gotten along well during our brief encounters, I wouldn't have said we were friends, and her wanting to speak with me certainly had my curiosity piqued.

I picked up two Manila folders from the table and left the compound. If my hunch was right, Jackie was ripe for the picking and I wanted her on my team.

~*~

I parked my car near the café where we'd agreed to meet and stuffed one of the folders I needed later under the passenger seat, out of sight. I gathered the other in my hand, stepped from the car, locked the doors, and crossed the street.

As soon as I entered the small café, my eyes zeroed in on Jackie, who was seated at a table in the back corner. She had an uninterrupted line of view to the door, and her eyes immediately locked on mine.

"Can I help, ma'am?" A young man dressed in black pants and a white shirt drew my attention.

"I'm meeting a friend at the table in the back." I indicated where Jackie sat waiting. "I'll have coffee—black."

"I'll bring it over."

"Thank you."

I zigzagged my way through a number of tables, some occupied, others vacant. When I reached Jackie, she stood and extended her hand. We said hello as we shook before sitting.

"Thanks for coming, Claire."

I noticed her eyes glance to the Manila folder I'd placed on the table.

"I'm curious as to why you wanted to meet."

"I heard about your family, and I'm so very sorry."

I nodded in acknowledgment and waited for her to continue.

"I also heard you left the navy on..."

"Unpleasant terms," I finished. "I was tired of the red tape, my hands being tied, and fucking assholes getting away with killing innocents because our government refused to step up to the plate. I um... sort of told them exactly that before I walked out."

"So, what are you doing now?"

The waiter placed a coffee in front of me, and after thanking him, I waited until he was out of hearing range and answered. Or rather, I questioned.

"What do you think I am doing, Jackie?"

"I have no idea, but I'm hoping you're doing something I can be a part of before I go crazy. When word reached me that you had hit civvy street, I was shocked at first, knowing you are military through and through. Then my gut told me you had something in mind and had the money to make it happen. Covert ops?"

I sat back in the chair; my hands clasped together on the table. Damn, the lady was good. I hadn't mentioned a word to anyone other than Tiffany, my contacts and *Bandit*. Jackie had a natural instinct, really knew people, and figured out how they thought, even if they'd only just met.

I nodded slowly and sipped at the coffee. "I'm putting together a covert ops team that, as far as public perspective is concerned, will be a security firm. I have a state-of-the-art compound ready to activate about an hour from here. I want to take out the motherfuckers the government has failed to take action against."

"You covered?"

"Usual—a CIA contact here for the more private of contracts, extraction and such, and a contact in Washington for non-sanctioned government work. Terms are what you would expect—anything we do will be denied if we're caught and we don't exist. You don't have family if I remember correctly."

"No, I don't," she snapped.

It was interesting how her demeanor changed at the mention of family, and I couldn't help but wonder why.

"Won't you get in the way of teams that already exist?"

"No, because my team will be the best, and if we do end up with the same targets, we'll be in and out before they zip their dicks into their pants."

Jackie laughed. "I see your opinion of men hasn't changed."

It was my turn to snap. "No, it hasn't. Are you interested because I'm in need of a third sniper?"

"For fuck's sake, do you really need to ask?"

I pushed the file toward her. "Read and sign these."

"Now?"

"Now."

"I'm guessing if I cross any lines with the team, my remains will never be found."

It was my turn to laugh. "I trust you to do the right thing, Jackie. I've seen your passion for justice firsthand, but yeah, cross me and your bones won't be found until aliens arrive."

"I won't let you down, Claire. I need this more than you could ever know."

I quietly sat while Jackie signed the papers before closing the file and pushing it forward.

"Welcome to the team." I handed her a slip of paper with the address of the compound. "Meet me here at three this afternoon and I'll show you over your new workplace."

I finished the last of my coffee, picked up the file and stood. "Will you have a problem leaving your job without giving notice?"

"I doubt it; let's say I'm not the most popular person in the place."

Jackie rose and engulfed me in a hug. "Thanks, Claire, for being a lifesaver."

"You're one of the best snipers I know, and it's me who should be thanking you."

Jackie sat back at the table, and after saying goodbye, I made my way out to the car. I'd barely buckled the seatbelt when a text I'd been hopeful of getting came in on my phone. It was Beth letting me know Nevada was at the stables. I started the engine and headed to where I hoped my next team member would be recruited.

~*~

I pulled up next to a candy apple red Dodge Ram, the metallic paint sparkled when drenched by the rays of the sun. After grabbing the file from beneath the passenger seat, I climbed from my car, locked the doors, and walked slowly around the Ram, taking in every detail.

I was my father's daughter when it came to vehicles—cars or motorbikes, it made no difference. I loved them all. I read loads of car magazines, salivating over the latest models and some of the unique features. The vehicle I was currently admiring had me licking my lips. It was the latest model—Ram 2500 Laramie 4x4 with a 6.7L turbo diesel engine. I almost groaned when thinking about that kind of power in my hands. Before I spent the rest of the day drooling over the mighty beast, I got my head back in the game and headed to the office to speak with Beth.

I found her behind the counter typing on the computer, and she looked up when I entered.

"Hi, Beth, thanks for the text."

"No problem." She didn't ask why I was inquiring about Nevada, which I appreciated. I would have hated to lie to her. "Are you taking King out?"

"I can't today, but I will be here sometime in the next couple of days. Is he out in the pasture?"

"Yes, I turned him out a couple of hours ago."

"Thanks. Do you know where I might find Nevada?"

"At the stables, she brought back a couple of rugs she had cleaned."

"I'll head down there; I have something to discuss with her."

"I'll see you soon."

I left the office, and as I headed to the stables, I caught sight of King in the pasture, head down and munching on thick, green grass. I smiled at knowing the magnificent gelding was mine.

I entered the stables, heard sounds coming from the tack room, and headed in that direction. Nevada was folding a rug into a box, which was pushed into the corner. I guessed it was her personal tack for Texas. She looked up, a curious expression on her face when I entered.

"Got a minute?" I asked as I made my way closer.

Nevada straightened. "What do you want?"

"I'd like to offer you a job... *Sissy*."

Nevada stiffened and glanced around to ensure no one had heard me call her by her real name. Her face paled, and she stared at me with wide eyes. Grabbing me by the arm, she kicked the door closed and pulled me further into the room.

"How the fuck did you find out my real name? Who the hell are you?"

I handed her the Manila folder, which had a copy of the email I'd received from *Bandit*.

She flipped the file open and read the top sheet, tears filled her eyes, and she sighed before placing the file on a shelf nearby.

"What do you want?" Her tone sounded resigned.

"I'm putting together a... security team, and I want to recruit you."

"Why?"

"You're the best shot I've seen when on the move, and I'm in need of a third sniper. I'm one and I've just recruited a second. Both of us are fixed position snipers. You give me options. I know some of your past—the most important details. I know you have high moral standards and can be trusted."

"We'd be required to go overseas?"

"Yes, but we would also have missions here on home soil."

"Where would I be working?"

"I have a compound ready for occupation about ten minutes' drive from these stables."

"My place is a small cottage not far from here, and I could stay there?"

"Yes, but you would also have a suite at the compound where you would be required to stay during mission planning before activation of the team. The rest of the time, you can come and go as you please."

"I can deal with that."

"Do you have a problem quitting your job?"

"No. I'll call and tell them something personal has come up and I won't be back. When do I start?"

I handed her a slip of paper. "I want you at this address at three and we'll talk further. I need these papers signed before I leave here." Picking the file up, I handed it back to her.

Nevada didn't hesitate. Moments later, the papers were signed, and the file was back in my hands. I couldn't help but muse over the fact that none of the ladies had taken any quality time to study the documents being thrust on them. It told me a couple of things—they were dissatisfied with where they currently worked, had a score of some sort to settle, and had a hell of a lot of faith and trust in my ability to put together a team.

"I'll see you at three. Thanks Claire. I think this may be what I need to move on in my life."

"The Ram yours?"

"Yep."

"Nice." I turned to leave and as I reached for the handle to open the door, Nevada spoke.

"Claire?"

I turned back to face her.

"I'm glad you picked me to help put the assholes of this world where they belong—six feet under."

"I look forward to getting to know you better, Nevada, and to working with you and your *security* team."

I left the stables, and when I reached the car, I placed the file on the seat. Pulling Jackie's file out from beneath the passenger seat, I placed it on top. Glancing at my watch, I saw I had two hours before both ladies were due at the compound. Time to grab a bite to eat and take another look over the list of possible candidates I'd been sent.

~*~

It was ten minutes before three when I arrived at the gates of the compound. The Ram I had admired earlier was alongside a royal blue, with orange racing stripes, Corvette Stingray—a car with fine lines and bucket loads of finesse.

I climbed from my car and headed to where Jackie and Nevada stood talking in front of the object that had snagged my attention.

"Ladies." I inclined my head toward the Corvette. "Yours, Jackie?"

Jackie ran her hand over the hood like she was caressing a lover. "Yep, saved damn hard for this baby."

I walked around the vehicle slowly, admiring the exquisite lines. "Year?" I had a good idea it was a 1969 model but asked anyway.

"She's a 1969 model."

"What's under the hood?"

"350 CID 435-hp V8, but you knew that, didn't you?"

I laughed. "Yeah, I did."

I crossed my arms over my chest and extended one leg in front of me. "When I left the navy and started on this team, I figured I would stay under the radar by not buying my dream car. Seems you two have blown that theory out the window."

"Which is what?" Nevada asked.

"The latest model black, turbo-charged, V8 powered GT Mustang with an all-black interior and Recaro seats." I cocked a thumb over my shoulder. "Instead, I bought that... *mom* car. Don't get me wrong, it's a great car, but not what I prefer. Guess what I'll be doing tomorrow?"

The ladies laughed, and I joined them before I had them sliding into their vehicles and following me into the compound. They patiently waited as I disarmed each gate and followed me across the compound to the warehouse, where we came to a stop alongside each other.

Jackie and Nevada joined me at the door and stood behind me while I entered the code to gain entry.

"Security isn't tight at the moment to make it easier to bring you in and show you around. Once I have everyone signed on and their information in the computer, it will be ridiculously tight, requiring eye and thumb recognition as well as codes."

I pushed the door open and stood back so the two ladies could enter. I followed them inside and watched as they examined the area, opening cupboard doors and admiring the furnishings.

Jackie headed for the door that led onto the deck, Nevada stepped up beside her. I unlocked it and both stepped outside. They stood eyeing the crystal-clear waters of the pool and hot tub before glancing toward the bar.

I pointed to the far end of the wooden deck. "That door opens into a fully-equipped gym. I'll give you a tour of the outside once I have the entire team together."

Jackie and Nevada followed me back inside and waited while I secured the door.

"You will work from this compound on rotation. When we are gearing up for a mission, everyone will remain here around the clock. Do you have animals?"

"I have Texas, but as you know, he is provided for at the stables."

"Jackie?"

"No."

"You will spend a lot of time here, which is why I wanted the place comfortable."

Jackie and Nevada glanced at each other before Nevada spoke.

"Comfortable? The place is like a private resort for the wealthy."

Jackie agreed.

"Come with me and I'll show you the suites downstairs. There are two floors of living quarters, Tiffany has chosen hers on lower level 2. They are all exactly the same, so you would be choosing the position only."

We entered the elevator and remained silent while descending to the floor below. I stepped out first, and as I had with Tiffany, pushed open the door to the first suite on our right.

Chapter Six

I waited outside the door, listening as the ladies discussed which of their personal objects would go where. When they re-joined me, smiles lit up their faces.

Jackie smirked and was the first to claim a suite. "I'll take this one."

Nevada pushed Jackie in the shoulder. "Hope you'd jump in my grave as fast." She turned her attention to me. "I'll take the one across from here."

"Okay, now to the good stuff. Come with me." We crossed back to the elevator, and once inside, I pushed the button for the basement. This time I stood back and encouraged the other two to step out first.

"Fuck me!" Nevada exclaimed.

"Wow!" Jackie shouted as she hurried toward the computer area.

The two of them walked up and down, examining the equipment while I stood back.

Nevada turned back to face me. "This is amazing, Claire. Any geek would think they'd died and gone to heaven when they saw this. No wonder you knew who I was with this kind of equipment at your fingertips."

I nodded. "I already have someone, and yes, they said it was a dream come true. The computer guru I am currently using in Washington found your information, although my new computer geek could have easily found the same."

I guided them to the strategic virtual planning table and flipped a switch. Lights flashed and it lit up like a 4th of July fireworks display. The ladies' eyes widened in delight as they moved closer.

"Touch interactive?" Jackie asked as she caressed it with her fingertips.

"Yes. Each of you will have a computer station, but the planning of missions will take place here."

"May we?" Nevada asked, indicating the table.

"Of course."

Jackie and Nevada spent the next fifteen minutes creating a strategic extraction from some made-up country. Despite the laughter and giggles as they swiped across the screen, I recognized the genius in what they were doing. I was impressed with how well they worked together, considering they'd only known each other for a couple of hours. It gave me a lot of faith in their ability to work closely in a crisis.

"Before we leave, I want to show you something that will have you both drooling."

They followed me across the room. I switched off the security and unlocked a three-inch-thick concrete door to the 'weapon's locker.' When I pulled the door open, their eyes widened to the size of plates.

"I can't believe this arsenal." Nevada was the first to run her fingers over the rifles and machine guns housed in vertical racks. "You have some of the very best here."

"If you have a favorite that isn't here, let me know and I'll order it in. While on the compound, all weapons will be kept in safes provided in the closet of your suite. They will be removed only for missions or training." I stepped up to the large room. "The racks are on rollers and slide to give access to other areas— racks and ammunition lockers. It's kind of like a large library filing system. If you push all the racks aside…"

"Well, f… if I thought the computer setup was awesome, it has nothing on this locker. This would be an ordinance professional's wet dream." Nevada certainly had a way with words and we burst into laughter.

"You could wipe a few towns out with this lot. What have you got in the way of grenades?" Jackie peered at the grenades lined up in boxes.

"There are about a hundred of everything– fragmentation, illuminating, chemical, offensive and non-lethal. There are two hundred training grenades and two hundred flash-bangs. Once you're inducted with the rest of the team, you're welcome to take a closer look. There is also a large selection of knives and close combat weapons. Try what you think would be your best fit."

"I have my own and would prefer to use them if you don't mind."

I acknowledged Nevada's request. "I expect a few of you will have weapons you prefer to use. As I said, keep them secure in the gun safe in your room."

"Jackie, your preference?"

"M24, Beretta M9 and Glock 9 for ankle holster."

"I have three of each. The first day the entire team comes in will be a day for induction, handing out vests, weapons and other requirements. Nevada, give me a list of the ammo you need if it's not already here." I pushed the shelves to the other side of the room, revealing floor-to-ceiling cabinets. "They contain ammo for every weapon in the locker and some for weapons I thought some of you might already have. Any questions?"

The ladies shook their heads.

"Okay, let's get you into the security system so you can get into the compound without me the next time you come out here. As you saw, each suite has a coded door, which I shall also provide a card for. After that, we'll go back upstairs and get you hooked up with a burner phone, laptop, and pager. Personal devices—laptops, phones, tablets are to be destroyed before you come back to the compound. You will be equipped with clean devices on induction day."

After they readily agreed, we took care of the current security protocol and headed upstairs. I removed the laptops, phones and pagers from a large safe room off the inside of the kitchen pantry and gave them each a card with the code to their suite.

I escorted Jackie and Nevada out before returning to my suite to study the information I'd been sent on possible candidates for the team.

~*~

Over the following three days, I spent time at the stables, riding and getting to know King. He was everything I knew he would be and tension melted from my body when we were together.

When I wasn't with my horse, I studied numerous dossiers, printed out information on the ladies I wanted to recruit, collated the papers into folders, and was ready to continue adding to the team.

Today I had scheduled a flight to Birmingham, Alabama, to meet up with an interesting lady who had been highly recommended by Alain.

I boarded the team's aircraft—the latest model Gulfstream G650. This was our maiden flight. At the top of the steps, I was greeted by Shaun Jenkins, my pilot, and Zeke Payne, the co-pilot. Both former military pilots in need of a challenge now and again. They would both pilot our Sikorsky CH-53K King Stallion on missions.

My target was currently employed by the FBI Human Trafficking Team in the city.

I settled into one of the white leather seats, ready to again study the information I had been given on Mackenzie 'Mac' Miller.

Zeke made an announcement from the cockpit as the aircraft began taxiing—my seatbelt was now to be fastened, ready for take-off. I clicked the buckle into place and gulped a mouthful of water from the bottle that had been beside my seat before focusing on the file in my hands.

Mac, as she preferred her friends call her, was of Viking descent—Norse Scandinavia. It explained the handle we suspected she used.

As a baby, she had been left in a box on the steps of the Roman Catholic Cathedral of St. Paul and the nuns had decided to raise her themselves. For years, she had suffered sexual abuse at the hands of each priest who had been appointed, as well as many of the church councilmen.

Using the cover of the FBI and their resources to find her perpetrators, it was suspected she was disposing of them one by one. It was the method she used to do so, which had me wanting her on the team.

She had been trained to strengthen her mind by one of the nuns at the church and could withstand the most horrendous of treatment.

Why the fuck hadn't she helped Mac to escape?

[81]

The training she received from the FBI in close combat had made her a lethal weapon, one I wouldn't want to encounter in a dark alley.

I studied the image in the file. Piercing jade-colored eyes jumped off the page and seemed to pin me in place. I felt as though she was looking directly at me. Her hair was jet black in color, some in dreadlocks with silver beads threaded throughout. A tattoo of angel wings on her forearm captured my attention, and I wondered what, if any, was the relevance.

I placed the image back in the folder and read the last of the information. Her weapons of choice came as no surprise—knives. She was even known to use a sword. Mac had also proven to be proficient with a gun, but close combat seemed to be her forte and was one of the reasons I wanted her.

"How's it going, Claire?"

Shaun took a seat on the other side of the aisle and I closed the file.

"Good. Hopefully, I should have the team together in the next few days."

"I'm assuming you're on your way to recruit someone?"

Shaun and Zeke had been told I was putting together a 'security' team but had not been given the details of what we would be doing. Having said that, both men were former military themselves and not stupid. It appeared the topic would be danced around to prevent any embarrassment. They would have no details on the missions they were required to pilot the helicopter for, they would be strictly need to know and both men were fine with the directive.

"Yes, I'm hoping I'll be able to convince her to join us."

"Good luck, she should be honored that you want her as part of your team."

"We'll see."

"We'll be in Birmingham in around three and a half hours. It should be a smooth flight, and we're not expecting any delays."

He stood to return to the cockpit. I unclipped my seatbelt and headed to a small galley at the rear of the plane, where I helped myself to a pre-packaged sandwich and can of soda. After settling back in the seat, I opened my tablet to the book I had been reading.

One of the main characters was about to catch the man he'd been in love with since college in the arms of another man. I predicted fireworks and couldn't wait to find out if the two friends would finally reveal their feelings for each other.

~*~

"Please fasten your seatbelt and ready for landing, Claire." Zeke's sensual voice entered the cabin via the public address system. It wasn't any wonder women were attracted to the tall sexy man with a voice that sounded as smooth as the finest of aged whiskey.

As the aircraft descended, I peered through the window and savored the view of Birmingham as it seemed to rise up toward us. Skyscrapers of various sizes were packed closely together. Parks dotted here and there reminded one that nature did still exist. The sky surrounding us was clear blue, but a thin blanket of haze hung over the area.

Birmingham, Alabama, had been founded on cotton but prospered thanks to iron and steel production. Both were major components in the railroad industry, and as railways had grown and expanded throughout the county, Birmingham thrived. It now ranked as one of the largest banking centers in the United States and was dominant in many areas, from education to medicine.

The wheels of the plane hit the tarmac as light as a ballerina returning to the ground after a leap and taxied to the terminal. When the seatbelt light flickered before blinking out, and Zeke opened the door, I stood, grabbed the file for Mackenzie, and watched as the steps were wheeled into place.

I glanced at my watch to see it was just gone half-past eleven. I'd be able to catch Mackenzie readying for her lunch break by the time I arrived at the FBI office.

I spoke to Zeke before descending the steps and heading off to locate a cab. "I should be back in three hours."

~*~

It was a little after midday when I walked into the downtown Birmingham FBI office building and met Alain's contact—Don Rossini, on the third floor.

His secretary escorted me into his office and introduced us to each other. She closed the door as she left and Don motioned for me to sit.

"Do I get to know what this is about?" Don was hoping I'd give him a reason for my being there. *Hope* being the operative word. He knew I would not be forthcoming.

"Sorry, need to know."

He smiled and shrugged. "Worth a try." He pushed a button on his phone and requested his secretary send in Mackenzie.

Moments later, a knock sounded at the door and the girl from the photograph entered. Her sparkling jade eyes locked on mine before she turned to Don.

"What's this about, Don?"

"Mackenzie Miller, meet Claire Marshall, the lady from San Diego I told you about who wants to speak with you."

She spun back and fixed me with a stare.

"Why?" Her tone was abrupt and to the point.

I stood. "Nice to meet you too." I ignored her glare and asked Don, "Do you mind if I take her to the café across the street? No offense, but I'd rather not have this conversation where the rooms have cameras and bugs."

"I was instructed to give you whatever you need... so sure."

Mackenzie stood with her legs slightly apart and arms crossed over her chest. It was obvious she had no intention of going anywhere.

"I'm not leaving this office until someone tells me what this is about."

I stepped forward and placed a hand on her arm. When that earned me another glare, I quickly dropped it back to my side. "Mackenzie, please give me a chance to speak with you. I think you will be interested in what I have to say."

She stood staring, deep in thought. This was a woman who didn't trust, and with a past like hers, I couldn't say I blamed her.

She nodded slowly and her body relaxed. "It's Mac and you've got twenty minutes." She turned to leave the office before throwing over her shoulder as she walked away— "lunch is on you."

I grinned at Don and hurried after the woman.

Chapter Seven

Mac, as she insisted, flicked a dreadlock over one shoulder, sat back in the chair, and crossed her arms. We'd already given the waitress our orders and were now alone. She sat waiting for me to begin speaking.

"I'm putting together a security team which will be based about an hour and a half out of San Diego. I want you to join us and come back with me."

"No thanks. I don't do security—spying on cheating men and women. Most of them get what they fucking deserve, I reckon."

"Neither do we."

Mac tilted her head and studied me hard. "Covert?"

I nodded.

"Why me?" Her eyes dropped to the napkin she was fiddling with between her fingers.

"I want your skills, your ability to move in close on a perp and kill silently."

Her head snapped up. "How would you know I'm capable of doing that?"

"CIA."

A flash of defeat crossed her eyes but disappeared as fast as it had appeared.

"They know about me?"

"Yes."

"San Diego, you said?"

"Yes. I have a large compound with all the latest technology. You'll have your own suite but can live off-site if you prefer."

"My targets are here."

"I know, but if you become part of my team, we can help you take them out quickly and quietly. We'll dispose of the bodies, and no one will ever know what happened... other than you and the team. You've made your point and most are running scared. They've gone underground and you're having trouble finding them. Am I right?"

"Yes," she conceded.

"We have the ability and technology to help you find them."

"When?"

"After I take care of one of my enemies first."

"What about my job with the FBI?"

"If you agree to my terms and sign the paperwork, my CIA contact will take care of your job. We'll also have your apartment packed up and everything shipped to the compound. Furniture can be..."

"I don't have any, the place was furnished. There are only my clothes and a few personal belongings."

"We can collect those on the way to the plane. Do you need anything from your office?"

"No."

"Anyone you want to say goodbye to before leaving?"

"Nope, but I have a car I want transported."

"Okay, I'll get it organized. Let's get to your apartment. You can sign the paperwork and we can have a late lunch on my plane."

"You have a plane?"

"Yep, it's ready to go at the airport."

"Well, fuck me! You must be some rich bitch."

I laughed at the expression on her face. "My father was the owner of Chatabook. When he died a little over two months ago, I inherited his estate. I sold the business and now I'm putting my own business together."

Mac laughed. "Business? Security company? Somehow, I don't think they're quite the right descriptions. Why do I get the feeling I won't exist once I join?"

I became serious. "Because you won't. Is there anyone who will notice you have disappeared?"

"Nope. I'm not exactly the type who attracts people to be my friend, and I suspect you already know I have no family."

The sandwiches and coffee we'd ordered were placed on the table.

Mac glanced at our order and shot me a pleading look.

"I think we'll have lunch first."

Mac smiled. "Thanks."

~*~

"Hi, I'm Shaun. I'll be your pilot this afternoon." He shook hands with Mackenzie before taking her duffle bag and large suitcase.

"Zeke, co-pilot." He also shook her hand before I tore her away from their drooling and led her up the steps and onto the plane.

When I reached my seat, I placed the briefcase containing Mac's file in a small cupboard nearby and indicated for Mac to take the seat opposite.

"So, this is how the other half lives?" She seated herself and fixed her seatbelt in place while I did the same.

"Ready?" Zeke asked from the opening to the cockpit.

"Take us home, Zeke, it's been a long day."

He gave me a mock bow along with an exaggerated flourish of his arm. "Your wish is my command, m'lady."

I laughed when he winked before taking his seat beside Shaun. The two men could be heard acknowledging each other as they proceeded to go through the pre-take off inspections. A short time later, we were speeding down the runway before lifting into the air.

Once the aircraft leveled out and the seatbelt sign was switched off, I removed my seatbelt and stood. "Feel like watching a movie?"

Mac unbuckled and rose. "Why not?"

I led her to a white leather couch in the center of the plane, which faced a large flat-screen television fixed to the opposite wall. A unit below had a large collection of DVDs in every genre.

"Take your pick." I indicated the unit with my hand before taking a seat on the couch.

Mac rummaged through the collection before holding one up in victory.

"The Notebook?" I was surprised she'd picked the romantic movie, which was one of my favorites.

"I love this movie; I must have seen it a hundred times but never get tired of seeing it over and over."

I explained how to slide the disc into the side of the television, and as it booted up, she joined me on the couch.

We settled in for a good cry.

~*~

Darkness had settled by the time we arrived back at the compound and I began the process of opening the gates.

"I still can't believe you drive this car," Mac stated for about the hundredth time.

"We can't all drive an Audi R8 V10, which wasn't what I expected, by the way. I really like it in matt black. Before you give me any more shit, I have a mustang on order, and delivery should be any day now."

"Good to hear. When you speak to your contact, tell him if his people put even the tiniest mark on my baby, I'll have his balls."

I laughed as I drove up to the warehouse, pulled the car to a stop, switched off the motor, and climbed out.

By the time Mac joined me, having grabbed the suitcase and duffle bag from the back seat, I'd opened the door and pushed it open. The lights flashed on, triggered by motion sensors.

"Nice." She glanced around. "I'm loving the kitchen. Do you cook?"

I burst into laughter. "Not if you want to be alive tomorrow. Chefs all my life. Rich bitch, remember?"

Mac laughed as she nodded. "I adore cooking, one of the nuns taught me in her spare time."

I held an arm out. "Have at it, the cupboards and refrigerator are well stocked. We'll eat and then I'll show you around. It will be nice to have you here." I was being honest. In the few hours since I'd met Mac, I was beginning to feel a bond forming.

Mac stepped through to the living room, deposited her bags and purse, and returned to the kitchen. I left her alone while I slipped downstairs to my suite, where I placed her file into a safe and changed into sweats and a tank top.

By the time I returned back upstairs, the aromas from the kitchen were positively mouth-watering.

I walked to the stovetop, where something bubbling in a pan was emitting aromas to die for. "That smells divine."

"It's a simple chicken curry with basmati rice. It's quick and easy but delicious."

"I'll set the bench."

Mac glanced around and seemed to realize for the first time that there was no table and chairs.

"We'll eat at the bench, and it's not as if we need a table for dinner guests."

Mac studied me closely for a moment. "I would rather we ate dinner at a table like civilized people, but this is your show."

"I'll order a large dining setting tomorrow."

"Thank you."

We remained silent as I set two placemats and silverware opposite each other on the bench before crossing to the fridge for a carafe of water. "Wine?"

"Please. Red if you have one."

After setting the water and two tumblers on the bench, I opened the pantry door and slipped inside. The room doubled as a wine cellar; one wall was filled with racks containing dozens of bottles of both red and white wines, ports and other fortified liquor. A fridge at the bar in the living area also contained a wide range of white wines as well as more racks of reds. Out poolside was more of the same. I selected a bottle of Justin Cabernet Sauvignon Paso Robles, two glasses from a cupboard, and took it all to the bench.

While Mac plated our food, I poured the wine, releasing the aromas of spices and black fruit into the air.

With everything set and a plate of steaming food before me, I climbed onto one of the bar chairs.

"This looks great, thank you." I moaned when I took my first mouthful. "Oh. My. God. I think you should be our designated cook."

Mac looked at me in alarm, a fork dripping food, arm frozen in mid-air.

"I'm joking. Once the team is together, our meals will be delivered, so all we need to do is heat them. A large freezer is due to arrive in the next couple of days. There will be plenty of ingredients for those who *want* to cook their own meals, so it's a personal choice.

"Why don't you hire someone?"

"Too risky. Covert, remember? The cleaning will be done by the team and any other chores that need doing. We'll work together on keeping the place clean and tidy."

"Understood. I'm used to doing for myself, so that won't be a hardship."

~*~

After we had eaten, I escorted Mac downstairs and showed her the suite opposite the one Tiffany had chosen.

"Tiffany, our computer expert, is in the suite opposite," I explained.

Mac had a quick look around before returning to where I stood waiting at the door.

"I'd like this one. It's close to the elevators, which is convenient."

"Consider it done. When we go back upstairs, I'll grab the code card, so you're able to keep it locked."

"I've got nothing anyone would want to steal and I wouldn't expect it from anyone you recruit."

"True, all my recruits can be trusted without issue. I shall give it to you anyway and it's up to you if you lock up or not. Come and I'll show you where we'll be working from."

Mac and I returned to the elevator and I pushed the button for the floor below. I didn't expect a great deal of reaction from her, it was nothing she wouldn't have been familiar with while associated with the FBI. Or at least that was what I thought.

"Fuck me. I thought the Feds had a great operations area; it's got nothing on this." She spun around. "All the latest, I'm guessing?"

"Yep. Only the best for this team."

"I'm impressed."

"Thanks. Let's go back upstairs, and you can settle into your suite, it's been a long day."

As I turned toward the elevators, Mac placed a hand on my arm.

"Thank you for this opportunity, Claire. I won't let you down."

"I know you won't. I wouldn't have chosen you otherwise."

Once Mac was sorted with the code card, a burner phone, laptop, and pager, I left her to get settled while I returned to my suite. There was more to be taken care of tomorrow and reading of files to be done.

~*~

The following morning, I heard the sound of the elevator doors opening and looked up to see Mac. I was savoring my first coffee of the day and studying the files for the day's meetings when she stumbled from the elevator toward the kitchen, having come from her suite below.

She was dressed in what looked like men's boxer shorts, the fabric printed in cartoon characters, and a white tank top. Her hair stuck out every which way, and as she stepped closer, I noticed she was bleary-eyed. A scowl on her face told me she was not a morning person.

"What the hell time is it, and why are you drinking coffee in the middle of the night?"

I glanced at the smartwatch on my wrist. "It's almost six." It was my turn to frown. "If you thought it was the middle of the night, why are you here?"

Mac grunted and grumbled before reaching into the cupboard containing a healthy supply of Ibuprofen, along with other first-aid requirements. I watched as she dispensed two of the pain capsules into her hand before crossing to the coffee machine and pouring herself a mug of the brew.

She returned to sit opposite me at the bench, tipped the pills from her hand into her mouth, and washed them down with a large gulp of black coffee. I wondered how she managed to do so without burning the flesh from her mouth. I would have preferred a cool glass of water, but each to her own.

"Headache?" From the look of pain in her eyes, I had a guess.

Mac nodded. "I always get a blinder the day after I fly. Doc reckons I get dehydrated, but even if I drink plenty, I still suffer."

"Might do you good to rest, maybe take a swim. I'll be gone all day recruiting new members, so help yourself to whatever you need. According to an email I received this morning, your car should arrive on the truck the day after tomorrow. If you feel up to a walk, the town is only about thirty minutes away. The fresh air might help with your headache."

Mac was free to come and go as she pleased now. I had set her up the previous night with entry and exit codes, as well as scanning her eye and thumbprints into the system. The only place that would be off-limits to the team unless they were accompanied by me was the weapon's locker.

I was pretty confident I could trust them not to launch grenades and obliterate the compound and nearby town, but I couldn't afford to take chances.

Mac continued drinking coffee with her eyes closed, rubbing the back of her neck while stretching her head from side to side in an effort to relieve her pain. When she opened her eyes, they looked marginally clearer.

"I don't suppose you want me to tag along?"

I shook my head. "Sorry, but if any of the recruits decline my offer, I need them to remain anonymous to others in the team."

"I understand." Mac climbed down from the chair, placed her mug in the dishwasher, and headed to the elevator. "Think I'll crash for a while, catch you later."

She stepped into the elevator, and the doors swished closed, taking her from sight.

I sipped the last of my coffee and gathered the files, along with my purse and keys. After dispensing with the mug, I set off to speak with my next possible team member.

Chapter Eight

My first 'target' for today was a member of the US Army SRT (Special Reaction Team), at least for the next couple of days.

Sargent Helga 'Hallie' van Staden's tour with SRT was ending, and she had refused to re-sign, which was why General Simmons had recommended her for my team.

The daughter of a South African Citrus Liqueur Distiller, and having an American mother, qualified her for dual citizenship—an asset that would be invaluable to the team.

She had told her commanding officer that she was leaving SRT to run one of her father's businesses in South Africa, something the General knew to be untrue. He suspected she had an ulterior motive—to go after her father and force him to reveal where her missing mother could be found.

With Hallie as part of our team, we would have what none of the other agencies did—eyes on the ground in the less than friendly South Africa, which didn't create suspicion.

I sped along the highway toward Fort Irwin, Barstow. It was an army base in the Mojave Desert, one hundred and seventy miles from the compound. While paying attention to the road and surroundings, I pondered what I had read in the file.

Hallie was not only proficient with several types of guns and rifles; she was also an expert in hand-to-hand combat. She was someone I could pair with Mac during stealthy incursions.

General Simmons had admitted he had a soft spot for Hallie after being on several operations with her and confided he was worried about her rogue attitude. He was convinced that once granted an honorable discharge, she would be on the first plane to South Africa, and he didn't want her risking her life. The general said Hallie had changed when her mother had disappeared, and authorities had refused to believe that her father was somehow involved. Even though they knew the South African had a history of kidnapping.

Hallie had excelled at SRT operations, including freeing barricaded suspects, hostage rescue, counter-terrorism, VIP protection, high-risk arrests, and counter-sniper assault. She had a wide range of skills rarely found in one so young.

My issue, and one of the reasons I would have ignored the recommendation had it not come from the General himself—her promiscuous behavior. The team needed to operate beneath the radar, and Hallie's less than stellar reputation with the opposite sex could place the entire team at risk. Nevertheless, I set my concern aside, hoping the benefit of having her on the team far outweighed the reason why I shouldn't.

I turned the car into the public carpark of Fort Irwin, and after finding a space, switched off the engine, grabbed the file from the passenger seat, and climbed out. After locking one file in the trunk, I secured the vehicle and strode toward the corporal on gate duty.

The young man stepped toward me, preventing entry to the base. "Can I help you, ma'am?"

I handed him the envelope from General Simmons. He took one look at the official crest and excused himself.

"Lieutenant Kidd is expecting you. I'll let him know you're here."

I thanked him and stood off to one side while waiting, fingering the ever-present folder in my hands. It wasn't long before a man about my height, thickly built, strode toward me with purpose. The corporal handed off the envelope and the Lieutenant continued to approach.

"Commander Marshall?"

"Yes."

"Lieutenant Roger Kidd, welcome to Fort Irwin." We shook hands, and he spoke briefly with the corporal before signing the security register. He then asked me to join him, and we made our way to an office building on the left after we'd cleared the entry gate.

"Sargent van Staden should be with us promptly."

I was shown into what I assumed was his office. I glanced around while he pulled two bottles of water from a nearby fridge and placed them on the desk in front of two chairs.

"Is there anything you need?"

"No, thank you, Lieutenant."

A knock on the wall by the door had us both turning. The woman before me had a bright pair of hazel-colored eyes, and sunlight, which streamed through a window, caused slivers of gold to shimmer and dance. I had never seen eyes so unusual.

Her hair was the dark auburn color of raging flames, and although she was short at not much more than five feet in height, Hallie had the streamlined build of an athlete.

I had seen the image enclosed in her file but was still taken by surprise with her youthful appearance. Her date of birth indicated she was in her early thirties, yet she looked no more than eighteen—*half her damn luck.*

"Sargent, this is Claire Marshall, former Navy SEAL. Claire—Helga 'Hallie' van Staden."

After the officer introduced us, we shook hands.

"As you know, Claire has requested to have a word with you."

Hallie shrugged. "You do know this is going to cut into my farewell lunch, Lieutenant."

Before the officer could speak, I did. "I assure you; this shouldn't take long." I indicated for her to take one of the chairs, and she sat, swiping the water from the table as she did. Bending one leg, she rested the ankle on the knee of her other leg.

"I'll leave you two alone. How long do you think you'll be, Miss Marshall?"

"Give me half an hour, which I'm sure will give the Sargent plenty of time to be at the mess hall before the festivities commence."

He smiled before leaving and closing the door with a soft click.

"Start talking *former* SEAL. I don't know why you're here, and frankly, I don't much care."

She was feisty this one, and I could imagine her going rogue. "Any leads on your mother?"

Her eyes widened in surprise before narrowing in suspicion. "I have no idea what you're talking about."

Opening the file, I removed the information on her efforts to find her mother and placed them on the desk before her.

She flicked her eyes over the paper before pushing it back to me. "How did you get that information?"

"I have contacts in Washington and the CIA in San Diego. Being of immediate South African descent, you didn't really believe your actions would go unnoticed, did you? If you agree to hear me out, I believe we can help each other."

Hallie took a large mouthful of water, settled back in her chair, and pinned her eyes to mine. "I'm listening."

I explained about the team, my intentions, and the compound. When I finished speaking, we sat in silence for a few moments. From the way she appeared to be mulling over what I'd said, I suspected I had captured her interest.

"So, you're telling me you'll be able to help with finding my mother? That I would have the support of your team and this computer whizz who can find anything on the dark web?"

"If there is anything buried on the dark web, Tiffany will find it, and we can put together a mission that will work. It won't be implemented until I take care of some outstanding business in Ailinia. Other team members have their own agendas also, which is the reason they have joined. If you are all patient and work together, we will take care of *all* your issues. I give you my word; we will do everything possible to get your mother back. It will just take time."

"Well, I wasn't getting anywhere on my own, and the authorities were doing shit all. I wasn't looking forward to confronting my father, so your team sounds like my best option."

"I do have one concern, Hallie."

She sat forward; arms crossed over her chest. "What's that?"

"I'm concerned about..." I searched for the right words so as not to upset her.

"Just spit it out, for God's sake."

There was that feisty, impatient side again. "I'm worried about your propensity for bringing men into your bed."

"I work damn hard, so I play hard too." Hallie stood. "If it's a problem, I'm sorry you've wasted your time."

"Please. Sit down."

She lowered back into the chair, returning the upper hand to me for the moment. "It's important we don't draw attention to our activities. If you want my help, you need to keep things discreet. You said you would live on the compound, so maybe use a local hotel or their homes for your activities?"

"I can do that; I never bring them into my own bed. Where do I sign?"

Despite my lingering reservations, I wanted the lady. Flipping open the folder again, I withdrew the paperwork that I needed signed and placed it before her with a pen. It took mere moments for her to scrawl her signatures and shove the papers back.

"I finish here the day after tomorrow. I don't have much shit to pack, so I'll see you at the compound at midday the day after tomorrow."

"Text me when you arrive and then we will dispose of your phone." She entered my phone number into her phone and we both stood. "I look forward to having you on the team."

A knock sounded, I called out to come in, and the Lieutenant pushed the door open. When he noticed us standing, he smiled.

"Looks like I timed it well. You all done?"

"Yes, we were about to leave."

The officer had no idea why I was there or what we had been discussing. General Simmons had ordered him to facilitate the meeting, and of course, he had complied.

"I'll walk you to your car, Miss Marshall."

Hallie led the way from the office, and after saying I would see her in a few days, I walked in silence to my car. After thanking the Lieutenant, I set out for home. There was another possible recruit I needed to see before the day was over.

~*~

On the way back from Fort Irwin, I stopped for lunch and called Mac to see if everything was okay. She assured me she was fine and said she'd had a workout and swim before relaxing and watching a movie. I told her I'd look forward to catching up with her at dinner.

It was a little after three in the afternoon when I pulled the car into the driveway of a small suburban cottage not far from the compound.

I'd called the former Marine, Jade Hawthorne, the previous evening, and she had agreed to our meeting, even though the tone of her voice alerted me that she was unsure and wary of why she was consenting.

Grabbing her file from the passenger seat and with Hallie's information secure in the trunk, I left the vehicle, locked the doors, which set the alarm and made my way up the steps to the front door, admiring the kick-ass Harley as I passed. My knock had the door being flung open almost immediately; I suspected she had been watching through a front window.

I came face to face with a woman I could only describe as Amazonian. My eyes climbed her body until I peered into brown eyes the color of molten chocolate.

The lady was tall. Her file had said she was six feet, one inch, but she looked taller. Long, curly brunette hair hung over one shoulder and brushed at her waist. A tattooed bat symbol adorned one forearm, and I suspected there was some deep meaning attached, which had not been mentioned in the information I'd been given.

Dressed in fatigues, combat boots, and with multiple ear piercings that glittered in the sunlight, she looked to be every bit the kick-ass woman I'd expected.

Proficient in Jujitsu, kickboxing, and boxing, along with her expert use of a Ka-Bar, the lady was lethal and I wanted her on my team.

"Claire?"

"Yes, that's me."

Jade stepped back, indicating for me to enter. Once inside, I followed her through the neat home until we reached the kitchen.

"Coffee? Tea? Water?" she offered.

"Water, if you don't mind."

Jade poured two glasses of water from a jug in the refrigerator and joined me where I stood near the table.

"Have a seat."

She placed one of the glasses in front of me before sitting in a chair catty-corner to mine.

"Tell me what this is about. You said you're a former SEAL?"

"Yes, I am."

"Why did you bug out?"

"I was tired of having my hands tied by red tape and watching murdering assholes get to walk away."

"I understand how you feel, but it still doesn't explain why you're here."

"I'm putting a security team together. The compound we'll be operating from is less than ten minutes by car from here. I have a contact in

Washington who will be advising us on missions and a CIA operative in San Diego."

Jade sat forward; her interest now evident. "Covert?"

I nodded.

"I'm interested. I saw too many good people lose their lives to assholes who walked away. I wouldn't mind some payback."

"Will you have any trouble with leaving your job?" Jade worked as a motorcycle mechanic, and it made sense since she also rode a bike.

"Nah. The owner is a good friend who was pretty much doing me a favor by giving me employment. I'll tell him I've taken a position with a security company. I think he only gave me the job so he could see my bike every day."

"The Harley V-Rod Muscle I saw in the driveway is yours, I'm guessing."

"Yep. I don't drive a car; I like the wind in my hair. When will I be expected to turn up to the compound? Am I required to live there?"

"I'll need you there in two days. You're welcome to continue staying here, but there will be a suite at the compound for your use. Do you have the time to come out and take a look around now?"

"Sure."

I pushed the file toward her. "I need the paperwork signed before we go any further."

I sat quietly, sipping at the glass of water and glancing around while Jade actually read over the documents before signing. Once done, she tucked everything back in the folder and pushed it across the table toward me.

"Let's go, I have an early start tomorrow. There are a couple of things I want to finish before I leave the garage." Jade stood, as did I, and I followed her from the house.

I stood watching as she threw one leg over the motorcycle and started the engine—a deep rumble filled the air. It was one sweet machine. She reached for the helmet hanging from the handlebars, and I climbed into my car. When she kicked up the side stand, I reversed out of the driveway and led the way to the compound.

~*~

Jade, Mac, and I stood near the kitchen bench, drinking coffee and chatting after I'd shown Jade over the warehouse. She'd chosen a suite on lower level 2 for when she needed to stay.

"You mentioned there are a couple of men you want revenge on to pay for the deaths of fellow marines?" I suspected the former marine had been exposed to some of the same carnage I had.

"Yes. I'll be able to utilize the expertise of your computer guru and team?"

"Once our first mission is done—the main reason for me putting this team together, Tiffany will be able to assist you with whatever you need. We'll discuss this in more detail when the team is together the day after tomorrow."

"What time do you want me here?"

"Anytime during the day, but we'll meet in the conference room at 1400 sharp."

"I'll be here."

"Security protocols will be upgraded once everyone is on-site."

Jade rinsed the mug she'd been using and pulled keys from a pocket of the fatigues she wore. I walked her out after ensuring she had both the card with the code to her suite, a burner phone, laptop, and pager, which I'd issued her with just prior.

I watched her start up the bike and ride away. After allowing time to be confident she had cleared both of the exit gates, I headed back inside to Mac.

"I like her," Mac stated. "Former marine, I gather?"

"Yes. A very good one and walked away for similar reasons to my own."

"I look forward to working with her."

Chapter Nine

After heating up a meal of beef marsala and rice for myself, I sat down at the bench where I had already placed two glasses of red wine. Mac heated up a Beef Vindaloo and joined me.

"Sorry, but do you mind if I read? I'm at a really exciting part of this book. Someone is going to try and poison the pilots of an international jet. If it crashes, more than three hundred passengers will be killed."

I laughed at her desperation. "Go ahead. I have a file I need to study before going back out shortly. We sat in silence, and while we ate, I read the information on the next person I wanted to recruit.

An image of Daisy Grace, former marine special forces, lay on top of several sheets of information. She had glossy brunette hair, which hung down past her waist, olive-toned skin and piercing green eyes that sparkled like emeralds. According to her profile, she was short, standing a mere five feet, three inches.

Daisy had been brilliant at her job, dealing with strategic planning for covert marine operations. It appeared she had a brilliant analytical mind.

My concern? She was a thrill seeker—an adventurous lady who wasn't afraid to take a chance. A notation stated she never put her team at risk with her actions, but could she be trusted to tone down her thrill-seeking ways?

Her team leaders over the years spoke highly of her capability in both planning, strategy, and pulling her weight out in the field. There had been many instances where missions could have been FUBAR if not for her attention to detail and exceptional tactical mind.

She had been honorably discharged after an injury to her leg had left her lame. Doctors had told her in no uncertain terms that she would never again walk without a prominent limp. This was something she had refused to accept, along with the fact she would spend the rest of her military life stuck behind a desk. Instead, she had taken the offer of a medical discharge.

Currently, she lived on a secluded property surrounded by woodland about a five-minute drive from the compound. She was also doing exactly what she'd refused to do for the marines. Daisy was sitting behind a desk as a receptionist for a cabin retreat in return for being allowed to live in one of the secluded cabins.

General Simmons had given me his assurances that despite her being told her leg would never recover, she'd worked hard to prove the doctors wrong. With a daily routine of rubs, massages, bicycle riding, running, and hiking, Daisy had managed to repair the damage and now appeared to be functioning to her previous high standard.

The general was also convinced she would be the perfect addition to the team, as well as a necessary one.

With my intention being to take the team into dangerous situations, many in foreign countries, we would need her exceptional talent.

After finishing my meal, and the half glass of wine, I disposed of everything into the dishwasher. Mac followed behind me.

"Did the plane crash?"

"Nah, the hero saved the day. Was touch and go for a while there, though."

"I'm headed out to meet someone, I shouldn't be late."

"I think I'll go downstairs and finish this book. I'll catch you sometime tomorrow because I definitely won't be up at sparrow's fart of dawn in the morning."

I laughed at her colorful choice of words, said goodnight, gathered the file, and set off to meet, Miss Daisy Grace.

~*~

I approached a small wood and stone cabin, which sat at the end of a rough driveway. Various species of trees surrounded it and a muted glow from within lit the windows.

An orange Ford F-150 Raptor was parked next to the cabin, and it would make a colorful addition to our collection of vehicles at the compound. As I climbed from the car, folder in hand, Daisy stepped out onto the porch.

"Are you lost?"

I continued to approach as she shouted.

"No. I'm here to speak with you."

"About what?"

I rested my foot on the bottom step of three, leading onto a porch beneath a bull-nosed roof.

"My name is Claire Marshall, former Lieutenant Commander with SEAL Team 3."

"Former?"

"Can I come inside and speak with you?"

Daisy studied me for a few moments before finally nodding and inviting me inside.

The cabin was warm and rustic. A lamp cast a soft light into the room from where it sat on a small side table. An open book, open and face down, rested beneath.

Daisy indicated the couch and I sat.

"Would you like something to drink?"

When I declined, she sat in the single chair near the table and lamp.

"To answer your question, I left the navy around two months ago—honorably. I was sick to death of having my hands tied. I'm in the process of forming a security..." I made air quotes to get my meaning across, "...team, to deal with the assholes who got to walk away after slaughtering villagers and other innocent civilians. The compound we'll be working from is about a five-minute drive from here."

"I don't understand why you're telling me all of this."

"I'd like your skills as a case analyst and strategic planner. You come highly recommended by a general I know, as well as your former team leaders."

"Why would they recommend me, especially a general?"

"He is very aware of your outstanding talent, and there appears to be a great deal of respect from previous team leaders for your ability."

"Hmm, small world, I guess."

"My main concern is your leg."

"There's no problem with my leg, the nerve has completely recovered, and the only time I have a slight limp is when I'm tired."

"You're sure it won't fail you in an operational environment."

"I can guarantee you that it won't. Tell me about this 'security' team. I get the feeling it's going to walk a thin line between legal and illegal."

"Your feelings are right. I have a general in Washington and a CIA agent in San Diego who will be recommending cases, but they will be off the books, so to speak. You have to understand; if you agree to join us, you will cease to exist. If anything goes sideways, they will both deny any knowledge or involvement. Is there any family we should be concerned about?"

"No, I was orphaned at the age of two, and no one turned up to take care of me. Before you ask, I don't have any close friends who will be asking questions. I like to keep to myself, especially after losing friends in action."

I continued explaining about the compound, and although I would have liked to have shown her the warehouse, it was getting late. She declined my invitation to visit the following day, saying she wanted the opportunity to clear up a few things at work before she left. I was concerned she may be leaving the business short-handed, but she assured me there were others who could take her place.

After a few minutes of thought, Daisy said, "I'm in. Where do I sign."

I presented her with the documents and she grabbed a pen off the table.

So far, everything had run smoothly with recruiting, and I looked forward to adding the last members the following day. With her signature on the paperwork, I placed it back in the folder and stood.

She rose and walked me out to the car. Before saying goodnight, we agreed to meet again at the compound in two days' time.

~*~

There was no sign of Mac when I entered the kitchen a little before six the following morning, not that I expected her to be out of bed.

I had three more possible recruits to speak with and wanted to get them all signed before the team met the following day. My car was due to arrive at ten, as was Mac's, so I would have to stop back into the compound after meeting my initial target.

While I gulped down my first coffee for the day, I typed out an email to Miles, aka Bandit, and hit send. I needed him to do some more digging on the person Alain had recommended and who was known only as 'Ghost.' The file contained some details I needed, but not enough. I picked up a photo to study closer.

She was older than some of the others at age thirty-five. Five feet, nine inches tall, and slender with thick brown hair. Her hazel eyes appeared to be focused on the camera, showed determination along with the pout of her full lips.

Alain had recommended her for her deadly skills with a gun and her ability to seemingly be invisible.

The familiar ping of an incoming email sounded, and I clicked on the icon to open the message. It had been less than five minutes since I had sent my email. The man was a magician. I sipped at my coffee as I read.

Claire

Info on Ghost as requested.

Retired from the Australian Army, and after a personal tragedy, relocated to the US.

I wondered what the personal tragedy might have been.

She currently resides in a small cottage, which she owns—address: 1527 Lane Avenue Borrego Springs.

It was a suburban location less than five minutes from the compound.

Known as Lexa Stone, she works evenings in her own bar-*Lexa's*. It's an LGBTQ+ bar downtown. She lives alone and prefers to keep to herself. She has no family.

Hope that helps.

Bandit

There was no detail on what, if anything, had happened to her family, and I wondered if she was alienated from them for some reason.

I stood, crossed the kitchen and placed the mug into the dishwasher. There was still no sign of Mac, so I scribbled a note letting her know I would be back in time for the delivery of my car and the arrival of hers. Both were due at 10 a.m.

Gathering the folders I needed, my purse, and the keys to my 'mom' car, I left the compound to go in search of Lexa.

~*~

I pulled the car to a stop in front of a neat but nondescript cottage and noted the late model red Ferrari in the driveway. Being a bar owner was obviously prosperous. The cottage was in a nice part of town and surrounded by other well-maintained properties.

I continued to admire the Ferrari as I locked the doors of my car, strode to the front door, and knocked.

After waiting for some time, I wondered if my assumption had been wrong, and she wasn't at home during the morning. As I lifted my arm to knock again, the door was flung open. A sleep-tousled, angry woman, dressed in sleep shorts, a tank top, and unfastened robe, stood before me. I didn't need to be a rocket scientist to know she'd been deep in sleep when I'd disturbed her. Oops.

"Who the hell are you, and what do you want? Do you realize what time it is? Even the fucking roosters are still asleep."

Attitude—I could deal with that.

"Lexa Stone?"

"Who's asking?"

I thrust my hand forward. "Claire Marshall."

Lexa glared at my hand like it was a snake waiting to extract a chunk of her flesh, so I dropped it back to my side.

"Can I speak with you about a security team I'm putting together?"

"Not interested." She began closing the door. I had a feeling she was going to be a tough nut to crack.

"Ghost?"

The single word had her freezing, and she glanced over my shoulder as if expecting others to be with me.

"I'm alone."

She flung the door back. "Come inside."

The invitation was issued grudgingly.

Once inside, she closed the door before grumbling, "I need coffee."

I followed her through to a kitchen with a small table and four chairs positioned in the center. Sunlight streamed into the room from the large window, through which the neat back garden could be seen. Dust motes danced in the beams which lit up the marble benchtops, causing them to sparkle and shine.

Lexa flipped a switch on a coffee machine and turned back to where I stood by the table, leaning her back against the countertop.

"Sit." She indicated the dining suite. "Coffee?"

She was obviously a woman of few words in the early morning. "Black, please." I lifted a chair, ensuring it didn't scrape on the wooden floor and leave scratches.

We remained silent while she fixed two mugs of coffee, placed them on the table, and dropped into a chair opposite.

"Tell me what this is about. If you think I'm going to run around taking pictures of men and women who have partners that have the money to set spies on them, you are sorely mistaken."

I liked her straight-to-the-point attitude.

"That's not what the team will be doing. Our missions will be taking out the seemingly untouchable assholes of the world."

Lexa sipped her coffee and raised an eyebrow. "How do you know about me, and how much do you know?"

"My CIA contact in San Diego recommended you. I know you're former Australian Army, and you relocated here in an attempt to move on from something that happened in your life. I don't know the details. When secret code 'tipoffs,' from someone code-named *Ghost*, started being received, the CIA dug deeper and found you."

Lexa again sipped at her coffee, studying me over the rim of her mug. This was a woman who didn't trust easily. After some time, she placed the mug on the table, wrapping her hands around the ceramic.

"Okay. You have me interested. Why do you want me on your team?"

"You're good with a gun and, more importantly—stealthy. While others are negotiating with assholes, you move in and take them out before they even realize what has happened. I need your skills."

"What about my bar?"

"The compound we will be working from is less than a five minute drive from here. Although many of the other team members will give up their jobs, I believe your bar could be a source of information. Do you have someone who can step in when you're needed with the team?"

"I have a part-time manager who could pick up the slack. I'd probably need to hire someone else to cover her when I'm not there. I could stay here in this cottage?"

"Yes. You will also have a suite on the compound to use when needed."

I spent the next twenty minutes answering her questions and watching her become more and more interested.

"I'm in."

I pushed the paperwork toward her, and after it was dealt with, she excused herself to get changed before following me out to the compound.

Chapter Ten

I left my car idling while I dealt with the gate security. Lexa had pulled up behind me in her Ferrari. The 3.9litre V8 engine rumbled loudly, breaking the quiet of the morning. Once the gates opened, she followed me into the compound and brought her car to a stop alongside mine.

As we both climbed from our vehicles, Mac—dressed in ripped jeans, blue tank top, barefooted, and with a coffee mug in one hand, opened the door. On spotting the Ferrari, she pushed past us, making a beeline for the beauty.

She floated her fingertips above the paintwork, respecting the unspoken code that you didn't touch someone's vehicle without permission, and circled to the open driver's door.

"Nice wheels." Mac shoved her hand toward Lexa. "Mackenzie Miller, call me Mac."

Lexa accepted her hand and shook. "Lexa Stone. What's your preference?"

"An Audi R8, V10. It should arrive on a truck in an hour or so, I hope."

"Sounds like a nice ride. I'll look forward to checking it out. Color?"

"Matte black of course. It would be sacrilege to have any other color. I'm sure you believe a Ferrari should always be red."

Lexa patted Mac's shoulder and pushed the door of her car shut. "There is *no* other color."

"Okay, ladies, let's head inside. Mac, I want to show Lexa around before our cars arrive."

"What's your crazy bullet?" Lexa inquired.

I had heard vehicles referred to in that way before. "A black, turbo-charged, V8 powered GT Mustang with an all-black interior and Recaro seats."

Lexa whistled. "Nice."

"I'll make coffee while you show Lexa over the warehouse." Mac headed for the coffee machine. She was developing quite the attachment for the hot brew it spat forth.

I took my time explaining everything in the warehouse as we moved from one floor to the next. Lexa chose a suite on lower level 2 before we continued down in the elevator.

When the doors whooshed open and we stepped out on the floor housing the computer equipment, Lexa darted her eyes toward me. I smiled as they widened. She was impressed.

"Well, I can see now why you're able to find people who want to stay gone. If I had a setup like this, I'd have been able to feed a lot more information to the authorities.

"We need everything it's capable of to track down the assholes we want to put out of business."

"You have a computer specialist?"

"The very best, in my opinion."

"I have to admit, I'm pleased you didn't turn and walk away after I hit you with my attitude."

" I don't give up easily when there's someone I want."

"Thanks."

I nodded and showed her around the room, including the weapon's locker before we headed back upstairs.

Mac looked up from where she sat, reading something on her tablet, and stood. She grabbed two mugs, poured coffee and set them on the bench alongside a small jug of cream and container of sugar.

Before taking a seat, I handed Lexa a code card for the suite she had chosen, a burner phone, laptop, and pager.

While Lexa added cream to her mug, I took a tentative sip of mine. The brew was hot and I felt it burn the length of my throat.

"What did you think?" Mac directed her question to Lexa, but before she could answer, we were interrupted by the blaring of a truck horn.

"My car!" Mac took off running. Lexa and I followed.

Mac released the gates and hurried to where the truck had come to a stop. The driver busied himself, releasing the straps that had held the vehicle in place for the journey. As I approached, my eyes flew wide when I noted my Mustang was also on board. I'd expected it on a separate truck.

When Mac's Audi was freed and secure on the ground, she signed the paperwork, accepted the keys, slid behind the wheel and started the engine. The unmistakable V8 rumble filled the air.

"Wanna come for that ride?" Mac leaned across to the passenger window and spoke to Lexa.

Seconds later, Lexa was in the passenger seat, her seatbelt buckled. I stepped up to the driver's door, and Mac pushed a button, lowering the window.

"I'll be out when you get back. I have another two recruits to speak with before the end of the day."

"Have a good one." Mac pushed the gearstick into drive.

[128]

"I'll see you tomorrow, Claire, and thanks again." Lexa gave me a finger wave as Mac turned the car toward town.

"Drive carefully," I shouted.

Mac waved a hand through the window as she drove off in a cloud of dust. I suspected she could be a bit of a lead foot when behind the wheel.

I turned back, and my heart skipped a beat when I found my Mustang was ready. After signing the papers and taking possession of my keys, I stood watching as the truck was driven away.

I drove back to the warehouse, grabbed my purse, the two files I needed, and hit the road in my new power machine.

~*~

I pulled up in front of *Ceps and Pecs*, a gym in downtown Borrego Springs where Bandit had informed me the next recruit would be finishing up a self-defense class.

Kelly Riddle, my first target for the day, was an Australian who had left their army and relocated to the US. I didn't have details on why she had uprooted her life in such an extreme way.

After snatching up her file and locking my vehicle, I made my way up the steps and into the gym. I found the woman, whose picture was secure in the file I held, talking with a young girl behind a reception counter. Standing back, I took the opportunity to study Kelly, who stood side-on, speaking animatedly.

She was tall, easily the five feet, eleven inches her bio had stated. Her dark brown hair was pulled back and secured in a twist at the nape of her neck. Escaped tendrils brushed the side of one cheek, which was visible. Her face was flushed, probably from the exertion of her instructing.

"Can I help you?"

When the girl behind the counter spoke, Kelly turned and gave me the once over. I suspected it was a habit she had, checking out prospective clients.

"I was actually hoping to speak with Ms. Riddle. I'm Claire Marshall."

Kelly raised her eyebrows. "Should I know you? Is this about self-defense lessons?"

"Not exactly. Is there somewhere we could speak privately?"

"Use the staff room, no one is due in for at least an hour." The young girl smiled my way. "I'm Gia."

"Hi, Gia, nice to meet you."

"Follow me." Kelly patted the counter. "I'll catch ya later, G."

Kelly led me along a dimly lit hallway before opening a door, which revealed a small room. Kitchen cupboards were fixed to a wall on our left, above a bench with a sink in the center and a coffee machine off to one side.

Kelly dropped a gym bag on the floor before reaching into one of the cupboards. "Coffee?"

"Thanks. Black. I'm not keeping you from a client, am I?" Miles had said she was free for a few hours, but something may have arisen.

"No. I have nothing now until four."

I liked Kelly. She appeared to be easy-going and confident. I hoped she would be receptive to the offer I had to present. I took a seat at the table, and once Kelly set two mugs of coffee on the table, she joined me, sitting opposite.

"Okay, what can I help you with? Are you looking for self-defense instruction?"

I hesitated for a moment. I hadn't considered that the team members would all benefit from her instruction. I had only been considering how we could utilize her skills to help us in the field.

While she patiently waited for my answer, she kept her eyes on the hand I had on the folder. I could see she was curious.

"Yes, I would like you to give some instruction, but first, let me explain why I'm here."

She nodded and the look in her eyes became wary.

"I'm putting together a security team and I would like you to join. I need your expertise with a rifle, gun, and self-defense. I have contacts in both Washington and San Diego who will be assigning... let's call them missions. I know you're former Australian Army and those you have worked with over the years highly recommend you for your exceptional covert skills. What I don't know, because the information I am given is need to know only, is why

[131]

you discharged and uprooted your life to come to the US."

Kelly's eyes narrowed; she sat back in the chair and crossed both arms across her chest.

"I loved the army, but thanks to my controlling, asshole ex-boyfriend, I was going nowhere. For reasons you don't need to know, he blocked every promotion I applied for and I couldn't take him dictating how I lived my life any longer. If I'd stayed in Australia, I was worried he would have eventually tracked me down."

"Does he know you're here?"

"In the States?"

I nodded.

"No idea, and I would prefer to keep it that way. I have broken off ties with everyone back home, so there should be no chance of him finding where I've gone. Tell me more about this team."

As we drank our coffee, I explained about the team I was assembling and my goals. I hadn't given a great deal of detail before Kelly sat forward.

"I'm in. Where do I sign?"

That had been easy. I pulled the papers from the folder and watched as she scribbled her signature in the appropriate places. Once done, I slid them back into the folder.

"Do you have time now for me to show you over the warehouse we'll be operating from?"

"Sure, lead the way." Kelly pushed up from the table and grabbed her gym bag.

I followed her back down the hallway and through the door that led outside. She pushed a button on a fob in her hand, and lights flashed on a dark blue Jeep Wrangler parked in front of my Mustang.

"That's my car behind yours."

"The Mustang?"

"Yep."

"Sweet."

I left Kelly getting into her car and slid into mine. As I passed her, she pulled out onto the road and slipped in behind.

~*~

Mac and Lexa still hadn't returned when we pulled up at the warehouse. Kelly left her car, gave the Ferrari the once over before scanning her surroundings as she crossed to where I was unlocking the door.

"The team is due to gather here tomorrow at 1400 hours and I will show everyone over the exterior grounds after introduction." I pushed the door open and stood back, allowing Kelly to into the kitchen area.

"Wow, this is huge." She continued through to the living area, crossed to the glass doors, which opened to outside, and peered through at the pool.

"Quite the resort." After glancing around, she turned back, a confused expression on her face. "Why the elevators?"

"There are three floors below here." I showed her into an elevator, pushed a button and we descended to the floor below. When the doors slid open, I directed her to the third suite on our right, pushed the door open and showed her around.

"I have an apartment in a building with a doorman not far from here. I've not long signed a lease; will I be able to continue staying there?"

"Of course, but you will also have a suite here for use during operation planning when we are working late. They are all identical, although some are taken. This one is available if you would like to make it yours. There are also some on the floor below if you prefer."

"I'd like this one."

"When we go back upstairs, I'll grab you the code card along with a burner phone, and pager." I closed the door, and we returned to the elevator, where I pressed the button to take us down to the basement.

Kelly whistled as she stepped out. The area seemed to have that effect on everyone.

"I thought ops rooms like this only existed in movies or in secret bunkers. I hope you aren't expecting me to know how to operate this stuff. You're in deep shit if you think I can."

I laughed at the look of horror on her face. "We'd be in even deeper shit if I was expected to know how to work everything. I have a computer expert who will have no issue with any of this equipment. Each team member will have the use of a computer station and you will also be issued with a laptop for use in the privacy of your suite."

"I'm guessing all current technology I am using will need to be destroyed?"

"You are guessing correctly. Download what you need to keep and ensure everything is disposed of as if it held top-secret material. All email, social media, phone accounts are to be closed."

"Gotya."

"Okay, I have someone else to meet with, so let's get back upstairs, and I'll issue you with what you need for now, including the codes and room card, the protocol for the entry gates, as well as a burner phone, laptop, and pager."

After issuing Kelly with what she needed and setting her up so she could gain access to the compound, I escorted her out.

Once back inside, I locked her file in the safe before starting off to recruit one of our most important members.

Chapter Eleven

After parking my car, locking the doors, and setting the alarm, I walked into *Maysons*–a café on the upper side of town. I had arranged to meet with Mae Jensen, a bomb handling expert who had, until recently, been a member of SWAT.

According to the information I'd been given, she blamed herself for being too slow to diffuse a bomb, which had resulted in a colleague being killed. From what I'd read in her file, the blame she shouldered was misplaced, but I knew she wouldn't accept it wasn't hers to claim. I hoped she would at least consider my offer to join the team.

Mae was one of, if not, the best in the business from what her colleagues said, and her expertise would be vital to our success.

A bell over the door announced my arrival, and as a waitress approached, I scanned the interior for Mae. I found she hadn't yet arrived, but as I was ten minutes early, it didn't cause me concern.

"Table for one?" The waitress plucked a menu from a stand near where she stood.

"Two, please. I'm expecting someone who should be here shortly."

She grabbed another menu. "Do you have a preference for where you would like to sit?"

The café was busy, but only half of the tables had people seated at them. I noted one which was tucked in a back corner off to my left and requested the position.

I followed the waitress, and while I sat, she placed the menus on the table.

"Can I bring you something to drink?"

"Water will be fine until my other party arrives, thank you."

She left to fulfill my request, and while she was gone, I kept my eyes on the door. Five minutes passed before a woman I recognized as Mae, thanks to the picture in her file, entered the café. Her eyes darted around the interior and I raised a hand to indicate it was me she was searching for.

I studied her as she explained to the waitress that she would be joining me and approached where I sat. Her bio had stated she was five feet, six inches tall and I could see that was accurate. Her long, dark brown hair fell straight over one shoulder. Hazel eyes flicked around the surroundings, ever alert. Her slender figure was encased in blue jeans, black shirt, and she wore combat boots on her feet. I stood when she reached the table and extended my hand.

"Mae?"

"Yes. You're Claire?"

"I am. Thank you for meeting with me today."

"I don't mind, especially since lunch is on you."

I laughed as we sat and pushed a menu toward her. She helped herself to water from a jug the waitress had placed on the table earlier and poured it into a glass. We sat in silence, perusing the menu.

"Ready to order?" The waitress held a small pad and pen at the ready.

I ordered a garden salad with chicken and a soda. Mae chose the chicken breast with salad, electing to stick with water.

Once the waitress left to give the kitchen our orders, I asked Mae about her intentions after severing her ties with SWAT.

"What have you been doing since leaving the force?"

"Not much, a bit of security work, but none of it was a good fit." She flicked her eyes to the folder, which sat on the table to my left. "I'm guessing you already know that along with a bunch of other information. You said on the phone that you're setting up a security team. I have to be honest; I'm not interested in spying on cheating husbands and wives."

"Neither am I. This team will be covert. Special Ops."

Mae's eyes widened.

"I'm looking for your skills as a bomb, grenade, and flash-bang expert."

"Diffusing?"

"Highly unlikely. It's more attack I'm looking for, to take out otherwise untouchable assholes." I took a deep breath. "I know you blame yourself for what happened on your last assignment with SWAT, and I won't even attempt to try and convince you that what happened wasn't your fault. I'm sure others have already tried. What I can do is have you look at what happened from a different angle."

Mae raised her eyebrows.

"Some asshole set that bomb in place with the intention of killing a lot of innocent people. Your actions reduced it to one. One too many, but one, rather than hundreds. From the information I've been given, the suspect has so far eluded the authorities. It's scum like him I want to shut down. Permanently. No court case. Lawyers. No chance they'll walk free on some technicality. I want them dead, so there's no chance they'll be able to hurt anyone else."

"It sounds personal."

"I have my reasons."

"Connections?"

"Yes. Washington and San Diego."

"Team size?"

"Big enough to rotate shifts if needed."

"Stateside or overseas?"

"Both."

The waitress placed our meals before us and handed me the check. As we ate, Mae described the dingy, flea-ridden one-bedroom basement unit where she lived in one of the less desirable parts of town. Her eyes lit up when I talked about the suite she would have at the compound.

She had no family. Mae's parents were both deceased, and she was an only child. She had also cut ties with previous friends on the force. She was riddled with guilt and unable to continue the friendships. It was a sad situation, but one that worked in my favor.

Once lunch was finished and the table cleared of dishes, Mae signed on the dotted lines, and I finished the soda.

Establishing she had no plans for the afternoon, Mae followed me out to the compound.

~*~

I glanced into the rear view mirror and watched as Mae followed me through the gates and pulled her black Jeep Grand Cherokee to a stop behind me. Mae joined me at the driver's side door as I exited the Mustang.

"The place looks impressive."

"Thanks. I'll show you through the building, and tomorrow, when we're all together, I'll show you over the outside."

I unlocked the door, noticing Mac and Lexa hadn't returned. Lexa's Ferrari was still parked where she'd left it, and I assumed they'd gone out for lunch. I hoped the time they were spending together meant they were beginning to bond. I wanted every member of the team to feel as if they belonged and had people they could count on to have their back.

Once inside, I showed Mae around the upper floor—the main living space. Like Lexa, she was surprised to see the elevators, having made the assumption the building was single story.

I explained about the three floors beneath where we stood and guided her to an elevator. Once inside, I pushed a button to take us to the floor below.

When the elevator came to a stop and the doors opened, I headed in the direction of my suite. Mae walked alongside.

Reaching the last door on the right, I pushed it open and stood back.

"All the suites on this floor, and the next one down, are identical. This one is available as well as a couple of others on this floor and some downstairs."

Mae stepped past me and proceeded to inspect the suite while I waited outside. When she returned, a smile lit up her face. "It will be like living in a five-star resort. I'm happy to take this one. Which is yours?"

I pointed to the door on the wall nearby. "That entire end is my suite. Owner privilege."

"As it should be too. Thanks. I love what I'm seeing and real glad I said yes."

"You're gonna love what you see downstairs."

I was excited to take Mae down to the basement. It wasn't the computer and strategic planning area that would have interest for her. No. Her interest would be what lay behind the concrete door of the weapon's locker.

When we reached the basement, I herded Mae straight to the concrete surrounded room and unlocked the door. I kept my eyes on hers as I pulled it open, and her reaction didn't disappoint. Her eyes widened while her mouth opened and closed a few times. Words eluding her.

Guiding her forward, I revealed the collection of grenades and flash-bangs before showing her the storage area I hadn't shown any of the others. There was everything needed to make low through to high-powered bombs.

Mae danced her fingers over the neatly arranged assortment of colored wires, connectors, fuses, timers, chemicals, pipe, dynamite and so much more.

Mae finally found her voice. "There's enough here to take out a small country. Or two."

"Impressed?'

"Uh... yeah!"

"Okay, let's go back upstairs so I can organize a few things, and you can go back to your unit and get packed. Do you need help with moving?"

"No, I don't have much. The place I'm in was furnished. If you could call a threadbare couch and lumpy mattress, furniture. I was on a weekly lease, so leaving won't be a problem."

"Why were you there?"

"I didn't want to eat through my savings while I looked for another job."

"Fair enough."

Once upstairs, I armed her with a code card for her suite, a phone, laptop, and pager. After familiarizing her with the gate protocol and instructions to dispose of all technology, I walked her outside to her car.

After she left, I headed back inside. My team was now in place. I needed to send an email off to Alain and Craig, informing them of my choices. Then, I was heading out to the stables for a well-earned ride on King.

~*~

After a brief word with Beth, who informed me she had been exercising King by giving him a good run every day, I made my way down to the paddock with the lead rope in hand.

When I reached the gate and called his name, King surprised me by trotting straight over. Nevada's horse, Texas, followed along with a couple of others I hadn't noticed before. I gave them all a pat before clipping the lead to King's halter and leading him from the paddock toward the stable block.

Once he was saddled, I hoisted myself onto his back. A click of my tongue, and a gentle squeeze of my thighs against his flanks, was enough to have him clip-clopping from the building.

Once clear, I gave him his head, and he raced over the ground. Wind had his thick mane blowing over my hands, muscles bunched and stretched beneath my body. He was magnificent in full stride and I found myself falling in love with the beast a little bit more. When we came upon the rocky ground which led to the river, he picked his way carefully over the trail. Once in the clear water, he lowered his head and took a long drink.

I sat soaking in our surroundings. I'd needed this after the stress of the past couple of weeks. I marvelled at how fortunate I'd been. Not one of the ladies I'd set my sights on had rejected my offer to join the team and I'd managed to get them onboard in half the time I'd initially planned. After our gathering tomorrow, we would be set, ready for training. Our first mission was drawing closer.

I'd been lost in thought and hadn't realized that King had retreated from the river and stood patiently awaiting my instruction.

Reaching forward, I patted his cheek. "You're such a good boy. How could anyone not love you?"

I turned him toward home, and after picking his way back over the rocky terrain, he flew over the ground toward the stables.

When we reached the building, I slowed him to a walk and guided him inside. After unsaddling and brushing him down, I secured him in his stall with fresh water and a large bucket of feed.

After giving him a hug and pat, I made my way back to the office, where I had a quick word with Beth before leaving to return to the compound.

~*~

When I reached the warehouse, I noted the Ferrari was no longer on the grounds, but Mae's dark blue Jeep was parked alongside Mac's Audi. I found both ladies in the kitchen and they turned to me as I entered.

"Coffee? I just made a fresh pot," Mac informed.

Mac and I might as well hook up to an IV with the amount of coffee we drank. It would be a more efficient way of getting it into our systems.

I dropped my purse onto the bench and hoisted myself onto a chair beside Mae. "Yes, please. I would love a mug. I've been out riding King."

"You have a horse?" Mae's eyes lit up as she spoke.

"I do. He's at the Coyote Canyon Stables. It's been a busy few days, so we went for a ride to the river. Do you ride?"

"No, but I love horses."

"You'll have to join me one day. They have several horses you can hire for riding. One of our other team members also owns a horse that is agisted there."

"I'd like that."

While Mac poured coffee, I continued speaking with Mae. "Did you get everything moved out?"

"I did. I'm out of the flea-ridden place and in comfort. I'm looking forward to meeting the rest of the team tomorrow."

Mac slid a steaming hot mug of coffee my way and climbed onto a chair.

"You and Lexa were gone for a long while, Mac."

"We drove down to San Diego, had lunch and chatted. I really like Lexa; she'll be great to work alongside. How about giving us the brief on the others?"

I laughed at Mac's natural curiosity. It wasn't the first time she'd asked me about the others over the past few days. "Nice try, Mac. Like everyone else, you will meet tomorrow."

She huffed out a sigh. "At least it's good to know we'll have some female support. Most of the other firms in the area are all macho males or have one token female for appearances.

I smiled inwardly. Mac and the others were in for a shock the next day.

I finished my coffee and left Mac and Mae to chat about some of their experiences while I headed downstairs for a shower before dinner.

Chapter Twelve

Most of the following morning was spent destroying the team files. I no longer had any use for them. I had also touched base with Alain and Craig for any last-minute instructions. It was then a matter of waiting for the ladies' arrivals. Mae and Mac had busied themselves in the pool, hot tub and gym.

The three of us had just finished lunch when I heard a vehicle driving onto the grounds. I had left the gates open as neither Daisy nor Hallie had been instructed on the protocol.

"Sounds like our first member has arrived." I pushed back off the chair. Mae and Mac joined me and we made our way outside.

Daisy was in the process of climbing down from her Ford Raptor, which she had parked alongside my Mustang. I was introducing her to the other two when Hallie arrived in a charcoal-colored Maserati Granturismo, closely followed by Lexa. This was it, the reality of my having an elite team was coming together.

Glancing at my watch, I saw it was a little after one. It appeared my ladies were all going to be early. It turned out I was right. The others followed in quick succession—Kelly, Jade, Nevada, and Jackie. Tiffany brought up the rear in the most impressive muscle car I had seen in a very long time. She parked the silver Shelby Mustang, accented with thick black racing stripes, next to Mae's Jeep. The area now resembled a luxury car lot.

"You have to be shittin' me. No men?"

I laughed at Mac's outburst. "No men."

"Well fuck me."

We all laughed at Mac's colorful language.

"Since we're all here, let's get started. Hallie, Daisy, I'll show you both over the building once the orientation is finished."

Both ladies nodded, and I led my team... *my* team... God, that sounded good, through the kitchen and living area to the elevators.

We split into two groups after I instructed everyone we would be going down to the basement level. The elevators came to a stop and we all piled out.

"Holy fuck," Hallie exclaimed as she gave the area the once over.

Daisy's eyes were wide with disbelief.

"The operations room." I clarified where we were for the benefit of the two who were seeing it for the first time. Not that they probably needed to be told.

We all gathered at the conference table where Mac, Mae, and I had placed jugs of water, glasses and plates of cookies. I took up the seat at the head of the table and waited while everyone settled. All eyes turned to me in anticipation.

"First of all, welcome. You have all been carefully chosen for the skills you will bring to the team. You are the very best at what you do, and that includes men. As I introduce each of you, I will give a brief explanation of your past and skills."

The ladies glanced at each other, and I swallowed a mouthful of water before continuing.

"Starting on my right is Jackie Ross. She is former Delta Force who I met when she was seconded to SEAL Team 5 for a few missions. Her specialty is her accuracy with a rifle and her stealth. Don't be fooled by her short stature and childlike looks. Speaking from experience, I can assure you, she's deadly. She will be one of our snipers. Her handle is FREYA. Like the rest of us, it was established in the past."

I paused while everyone welcomed Jackie.

"Next to Jackie is another of our expert snipers, but where Jackie and I are expert fixed position shooters, Nevada Phillips is deadly accurate while on the move. I witnessed this accuracy as she shot targets dead center from the back of a moving horse. Nevada was a US Deputy Marshall in the past and she goes by the handle—LONESTAR."

I sucked down some water while Nevada was welcomed.

"Up next is a lady we will all rely on very heavily—Mae Jensen. Mae was a member of SWAT and her expertise is explosives. She will cover our backs during extractions by creating diversions. Her handle is NITE—short for IGNITE.

Beside her is Kelly Riddle, another Australian who has settled here in the US. She was a member of the army, and although proficient with most weapons, her real skill lies in hand-to-hand combat. She will be instructing us in self-defense. Her handle is RIDDLE."

I took another mouthful of water, waiting while they received their welcomes.

"Lexa Stone—you were my biggest challenge, and I was afraid you would be my only rejection." I glanced around the table. "Lexa is another Australian who was also army. She has a ton of attitude and the ability to seemingly disappear into thin air. Lexa is accurate with any type of gun and her handle of GHOST is certainly appropriate."

Lexa gave everyone a stiff nod.

"The lady to Lexa's right is the person who has us all feeling vertically challenged—Jade Hawthorne."

The shorter ladies of the group all grumbled about Jade having been given the extra inches that they'd been denied. Once the laughter settled, I continued.

"Jade is proficient in Jujitsu, boxing and kickboxing, and I expect she will assist Kelly with self-defense instruction."

When I glanced at Jade, she nodded her agreement.

"Jade was with the US Marine Corp. She is both fit and deadly. Despite her size, her targets won't know she's coming before they're a crumpled, bloody mess on the ground. Her weapon of choice is a Ka-Bar, but she's no slouch with a gun. She rides the Harley you were all admiring as you passed. Her handle is HAWK."

Jade accepted her welcome to the team.

"Helga van Staden, who prefers to be called Hallie, is going to be invaluable when our missions take place on South African soil. Her father is a native of the country, and she speaks the language fluently. Her skills are numerous and varied. Skills she acquired while she was with the US Army Special Reaction Team. Hallie is feisty, willing to take calculated risks, and doesn't take shit from anyone. Her handle is HELLFIRE."

I could see the others were keen to know more about Hallie's interesting heritage. I wondered how much she would be prepared to reveal.

"The lady with the beaded dreadlocks and angel tattoo is Mackenzie Miller. She prefers Mac. This lady is of Viking descent, so it comes as no surprise that her weapons of choice are a knife or sword. I recruited her from Alabama, where she was with the FBI. Mac is the only one who has had the privilege of flying in the company plane. Her handle is FORSETI—God of Justice in Norse Mythology."

The other ladies were intrigued with Mac and I knew they would be questioning her later also.

"As important and vital as you all are to the success of my team, our next two ladies are crucial. First—Daisy Grace. She was with the Marine Special Forces and is proficient with most weapons. So what makes her special, you ask? Daisy has a mind for strategic planning and case analysis that is unparalleled. Add to that the fact she has no apparent fear of anything or any situation, and she is one incredibly deadly addition. Daisy is definitely someone we want and *need* on our side if we are to be successful. Her handle is DAREDEVIL."

I finished my glass of water and poured another.

"Tiffany Hunter is beside Daisy and I anticipate they will work closely together. Tiffany is the second-best computer hacker I know—the best being Miles Williams in Washington. He's the man who gathered the information on each of you. I don't expect she will be second best for very long. Miles will be arriving tomorrow and will bring Tiffany up to speed. She was with Quantico, which tells you she has a brilliant mind. She will be paramount to locating and keeping track of our targets. Her hacker name/handle is GLINDA. Tiffany is the person you will liaise with if you have any computer issues."

I waited while everyone welcomed the shyest member of our group.

"Last is me—your fearless leader or 'rich bitch' as I have been called." That comment elicited the laughter I expected. "As you all know, I was a Lieutenant Commander with SEAL Team 3. I pretty much left in anger when our last mission to take down an asshole terrorist—Ali Akbar Jabbar, was called off as I was about to pull the trigger and send the fucker into the afterlife in a million pieces. The result of our pullback was a village full of dead innocents. Taking him out will be our first mission to be planned over the next three months I want Jabbar, and his cohorts blown to fucking smithereens. My specialty is as a sniper, but I'm an expert with handguns, rifles and machine guns."

I sucked in a deep breath and ran a hand over my face.

"The money for this group is some of what I inherited. Just before I left Ailinia to return stateside, my father, founder and owner of Chatabook, along with my mother, brother, and sister were killed in a car accident. Two months ago, I sold the business and immediately began on this compound. I have one contact in Washington who is a senior defense member, and the other is an active CIA agent in San Diego. They will feed us information on any 'problems' that need to be eliminated but who they can't touch. If any of us are captured on a mission, any knowledge of who we are will be denied. From this moment in time, we do not exist to the outside world. So, before we indulge in coffee upstairs and I show you over the exterior, let me welcome you all. Damn, why are you all so fucking beautiful?"

They all burst into laughter, and I waited for quiet before finishing.

"My handle, which is new, is PHOENIX. Ladies, welcome to PHOENIX FORCE. Our motto? *Communicatio Illa Justitia*—Latin for Sharing of Justice.

I stood, and for a few moments, we milled about. "Hallie, Daisy, while the others go upstairs, we'll get your suites sorted."

The elevator we chose stopped at the lower level 1, and while the others continued to the ground floor, I showed Hallie and Daisy a suite. They made their choices, and we made our way to ground level, where we joined the rest of the team.

~*~

I gave Hallie and Daisy the code cards for their suites, along with a phone, laptop, and pager, before leading everyone outside to the gym.

Both the pool area and well-equipped gym were hits with the team. While they gathered around in the gym, I crossed to a bank of cupboards on the back wall.

"As you can see, there are lockers here for your use." I pointed to a door off to one side. "Through that door are six showers, six toilets and six sinks, so you don't need to go back to your suite after a session."

I pulled open two doors of a cupboard that revealed dozens of Molle Vests in plastic wrappers, neatly stacked in various sizes. "If your size isn't here, let me know, and I'll ensure it's purchased." I opened the next two doors. "The same goes for these helmets." The next section held backpacks. "When we go back inside, you'll be issued with a tablet, earpieces, and communication devices. After dinner, we'll go down to the weapon's locker where you can choose your weapons—gun, rifle, machine gun, or knives, along with ammo. These are to be stored in the safe in your suite unless we are on a mission or training. Communication on missions is to be by handle only. Any questions?"

A few no's were murmured along with the shaking of heads.

"Okay, let's continue." We walked across the pool deck and down three steps onto the ground before covering another one hundred yards to our left.

"As you can see, this is a mock village for training purposes. Most of you would be familiar with something similar, but this is the latest technology. The buildings can be moved by the push of a button to create various scenarios. We will use this to replicate plans for hostage rescue and straight-up firefights where we'll only have a split second to ascertain who are innocents."

As we walked two hundred yards to our right, Lexa asked how much land the compound encompassed.

"Two hundred and sixty acres." I brought the ladies to a stop at the state-of-the-art firing range, which elicited a number of comments about pretending the targets were one of the fuckers they wanted to take down.

I chuckled. It was exactly how I felt about Jabbar.

Moving on, we crested a low hill, and I pointed to the bushland beyond that covered the side of a steep hill.

"We'll be training with full packs on a trail I've had marked out. There are numerous obstacles, including sandpits, vertical walls, water hazards... you get the picture. Most of us have trained on the same kind of course."

I sympathized with their groans—obstacle course training was a long way from being a favorite of mine, but it was necessary.

"I hear you, ladies, but we need to be at the peak of our fitness, accuracy, and sharpness. We have only ourselves to depend on to stay safe. There will be no cavalry coming to the rescue. We have three months before we leave for Ailinia and during that time, we will be working a lot of twelve-hour days. We need to operate as one. There is *no* margin for error."

Everyone nodded in agreement.

"We are *Phoenix Force*, ladies, and the assholes of the world have no idea what is about to hit them."

I held a hand out in front, and the other members placed theirs over the top before thrusting their other arms high and shouting *Phoenix Force* into the air. It was the beginning of our journey. A journey I knew in my heart was one destined for success.

Want to know the full story of each team member?

Continue on for a preview of the ladies of Phoenix Force.

NOTE: Each book is a standalone read.

PHOENIX FORCE SERIES

BOOK 1—THE PREQUEL
Susan Horsnell
Release Date: 28 January 2022

AMAZON US

AMAZON UK

AMAZON AU

AMAZON CA

Read about where the team began.
Introducing the members of PHOENIX FORCE

BOOK 2—PAYBACK PHOENIX STYLE

Susan Horsnell

Release Date: 18 February 2022

AMAZON US

AMAZON UK

AMAZON AU

AMAZON CA

Character: Claire Marshall

Retired: Ex Lieutenant Commander SEAL Team 3

Vehicle: Black Ford Mustang

Position: Team Leader, Sniper

Handle: PHOENIX

BOOK 3—HIDDEN BOMBS
Lilliana Rose
Pre-Order: 4 March 2022
Release: 18 March 2022
AMAZON US
AMAZON UK
AMAZON AU
AMAZON CA

Character: Mae Jensen
Retired: SWAT
Vehicle: Black Jeep Grand Cherokee
Position: Explosives Expert
Handle: NITE (IGNITE)

BOOK 4—KELLY'S JUSTICE

Suzi Love

Pre-Order: 25 March 2022

Release Date: 8 April 2022

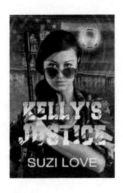

Character: Kelly Riddle

Retired: Australian Army

Vehicle: Dark Blue Jeep Wrangler

Position: Martial Arts Expert

Handle: RIDDLE

BOOK 5—FREE REIN
D'Ann Lindun
Pre-Order: 15 April 2022
Release Date: 29 April 2022

Character: Nevada Phillips
Retired: US Deputy Marshall
Vehicle: Red Dodge Ram
Position: Sniper
Handle: LONESTAR

BOOK 6—BAD BLOOD
Gemma Arlington
Pre-Order: 6 May 2022
Release Date: 20 May 2022

Character: Daisy Grace
Retired: Marine Special Forces
Vehicle: Orange/Black Wheels Ford F-150 Raptor
Position: Case Analyst
Handle: DAREDEVIL

BOOK 7—BLACK MASS

Aleisha Maree
Pre-Order: 27 May 2022
Release Date: 10 June 2022

Character: Mackenzie (Mac) Miller
Retired: FBI
Vehicle: Matt Black Audi R8 V10
Position: Knife/Sword Expert
Handle: FORSETI (God of Justice in Norse Mythology)

BOOK 8—RISE UP
Rebecca Barber
Pre-Order: 17 June 2022
Release Date: 1 July 2022

Character: Jade Hawthorne
Retired: US Marine Corp
Vehicle: Harley Davidson V Rod Muscle
Position: Hand to Hand Combat and KA-BAR Expert
Handle: HAWK

BOOK 9—HELLFIRE
Vi Summers
Pre-Order: 8 July 2022
Release Date: 22 July 2022

Character: Helga (Hallie) van Staden

Retired: US Army Special Reaction Team

Vehicle: Charcoal Gray Maserati Granturismo

Position: Expert in Extraction and Hostage Negotiation

Handle: HELLFIRE

BOOK 10—PHANTOM WARRIOR

J. O Mantel

Pre-Order: 29 July 2022

Release Date: 12 August 2022

Character: Lexa Stone

Retired: Australian Army

Vehicle: Red Ferrari

Position: Stealth and Gun Expert

Handle: GHOST

BOOK 11—ENDLESS REGRETS
K.S. Freyson & Kinley Crain
Pre-Order: 19 August 2022
Release Date: 2 September 2022

Character: Tiffany Meadows
Retired: QUANTICO
Vehicle: Silver/Black Racing Stripes Shelby Mustang
Position: Computer Expert
Handle: GLINDA

BOOK 12—FREYA'S REVENGE
JA Lafrance
Pre-Order: 9 September 2022
Release Date: 23 September 2022

Character: Jackie Ross

Retired: DELTA

Vehicle: Corvette Stingray 1969— Royal Blue with Orange Racing Stripes

Position: Sniper

Handle: FREYA

About the Author

Susan R. Horsnell is the new pen name for her steamy MF romance from mild to hot. As this cover was already processed, it will remain under the name— Susan Horsnell.

In Steamy Romance books, strong social themes are a feature.

She grew up in Manly, NSW, Australia and has travelled Australia and the World on postings with her Naval Officer husband of 47 years.

She lives with her husband, and fur baby – Gemma-Jean, a one-year-old Jack Russell Terrier, in a small village in the mountains in Queensland, Australia.

Since retiring a nursing career of 37 years, she has been able to indulge her passion for writing.

The family enjoys travelling the country with their RV when not at home renovating.

Author Links

SUSAN R. HORNELL

Web:

https://horsnells.wixsite.com/steamyromance

Facebook:

https://www.facebook.com/susanrhorsnellauthorofsteamyromance

Linktree:

https://linktr.ee/SusanRHorsnell

Email:

susanrhorsnellsteamyromance@gmail.com

Newsletter:

http://eepurl.com/hyPb5L

SUSAN HORSNELL

Linktree

https://linktr.ee/SusanHorsnell

OLIVIA ELLEN TURNER

No 1 Best Selling Author

Website:

https://oliviaturnerlgbtqa.wixsite.com/author

Facebook:

https://www.facebook.com/OliviaTurnerRA/

Amazon Author Page:

https://www.amazon.com/-/e/B09M32Y5CM

Linktree:

https://linktr.ee/OliviaTurner

Email:

oliviaturnerlgbtqauthor@gmail.com